Men ~ Bonus Edition

The Cabin in the Deep Dark Woods

Tim Barker

Book # _____

II Corinthians 3:3

Ye Three Men ~ Bonus Edition—This book contains the complete manuscript of the Ye Three Men story.
Published by Tim Barker
Published in New Port Richey, FL 34654, U.S.A.

All scripture is taken from the New King James Version® unless otherwise noted. Copyright © 1982 by Thomas Nelson. Used by permission. All rights reserved.

Scripture quotations marked [TLB] are taken from The Living Bible copyright © 1971. Used by permission of Tyndale House Publishers, Carol Stream, Illinois 60188. All rights reserved.

Scripture quotations marked [NLT] are taken from the Holy Bible, New Living Translation, copyright © 1996, 2004, 2007, 2013. Used by permission of Tyndale House Publishers, Inc., Carol Stream, Illinois 60188. All rights reserved.

Copyright © 2021 By Timothy L. Barker
Cover Design: Tim Barker
Original cover photo by Robert Murray
Editor: Bonnie Olsen

Table of Contents

Dedication v

II Corinthians 3:3 v

Preface vi

About this Book ix

Chapter 1 1

The Price of Shoes 1
   Scriptures: 5

Chapter 2 6

The Wounded Man in the Way 6
   Scriptures: 11

Chapter 3 12

An Enemy Amongst the Wheat 12
   Scripture: 16

Chapter 4 17

The Wedding Invitation 17
   Scriptures: 21

Chapter 5 22

The Wedding Garment Store 22
   Scriptures: 28

Chapter 6 29

The Marriage Feast of the Lamb 29
    Scriptures: 33

Chapter 7. .... **34**
  Every Knee Shall Bow 34
    Scriptures: 38

The Cabin in the Deep Dark Woods ~ The first four chapters only. **40**

Chapter 1 ~ Friday **41**
  The Journey Begins 41

Chapter 2 ~ Friday **48**
  That Treasure Chest 48

Chapter 3 ~ Saturday **54**
  An Ancient Scroll 54

Chapter 4 ~ Saturday **61**
  The Wise Took Oil 61

The Cabin in the Deep Dark Woods 2 ~ The first four chapters only. **66**

Chapter 1 ~ Saturday **67**
  On a Hill Far Away 67

Chapter 2 ~ Sunday **71**
  Mr. and Mrs. Peterson 71

Chapter 3 ~ Sunday **75**

The John Deere	*75*
Chapter 4 ~ Monday	**79**
The Rocks Cry Out	*79*
Appendix A	**85**
The Minister of the Holy Spirit	*85*
The Holy Spirit on Training Wheels	85
Appendix B	**92**
Non-Believer's Challenge	*92*
A Sixty-Day Study	92
Appendix C	**94**
Suicide Journal	*94*
Instruction to the Way of Life	94
Thank You from the Author	**99**

Dedication

This book is dedicated to my wife Jilean, our four grown children and their spouses, and our grandchildren.

II Corinthians 3:3

Clearly you are an epistle of Christ, ministered by us, written not with ink but by the Spirit of the living God, not on tablets of stone but on tablets of flesh, that is, of the heart.

Preface

Ye Three Men was originally part of the first book in the series: *The Cabin in the Deep Dark Woods*. It did not fit the storyline and was subsequently removed. It only had three chapters (chapters 1, 4, and 6). After pulling it out of the deleted file, I added four more chapters, turning it into a novella. This little book is intended to press upon the hearts of all the necessity to be born again.

I was inspired to write *The Cabin in the Deep Dark Woods* while listening to Jonathan Edwards's 1741 sermon *Sinners in the Hands of an Angry God*. Afterward, I thought, "Someone needs to write a story where God shows people who they really are from His perspective." That thought inspired me to write that first book and subsequently turn it into a series.

In 1741 both Jonathan Edwards and George Whitfield preached that people must be born again. But, whether or not you have been born again, this book will challenge your theology by opening the Bible, presenting God's truth to your heart.

Have you ever wondered what it means to be born again? In John chapter 3, Jesus discussed this topic with a man named Nicodemus. In John 3:3, Jesus said for a person to see the Kingdom of God, they must be born again. And then again in John 3:5, to enter into the Kingdom of God, a person must be born of the water and of the Spirit.

In John 3:3, the statement *"born again"* is a general statement. Nicodemus didn't understand what Jesus said, so in John 3:5, Jesus broke the general statement into two

components. The born of the Spirit part is simple, and that is a person must be born of the Holy Spirit. See John 15:26-27, John 14:25-26. It is the *"born of the water"* part that needs explaining. The best place to start understanding *"born of the water"* is John 4:6-15, where Jesus said, *"But the water that I shall give him will become in him a fountain of water springing up into everlasting life."* The question that needs to be asked: What does it mean to be born of the water? Read the following passages and remember Jesus oftentimes utilizes the Old Testament to bring understanding to the New Testament. The following passages highlight the living water:
1) Revelation 22:1-2
2) John 4:6-15
3) Ezekiel 47:1-9
4) Revelation 21:6
5) Jeremiah 17:13

Before explaining the scriptures above, I must explain that the water Jesus refers to in John 3:5 is not baptism. The only component of the born again process that relies on mankind is sharing the gospel message. The water that people are baptized in is of the earth. (Romans 10:15-17, Ephesians 4:11-16, Genesis 3:17, John 3:23). Born again is also called—born from above or born of God. The things from above are not mingled with the things of the earth (Hebrews 8:1-13).
1) Revelation 22:1-2, this water originates at the Lamb and then proceeds from the Lamb's throne.
2) John 4:6-15, this water is living water. Jesus distinguishes between the natural water found in

the well and the fountain of water that springs into everlasting life.
3) Ezekiel 47:1-9, this water is flowing from the temple of God.
4) Revelation 21:6, Jesus will give of the fountain of the water of life freely to everyone who thirsts.
5) Jeremiah 17:13, the Lord is the fountain of living waters.

Jesus had expected Nicodemus, a teacher in Israel, to understand that the subject—born again was an Old Testament standard. See the following passages on born again:
1) Ezekiel 36:25-27
2) Isaiah 44:3-4
3) {Jeremiah 31:33 & Hebrews 8:10}
4) Psalms 51:7

In conclusion, I must state, to be born again/born of God also means that a person has been cleaned from all their filthiness of the flesh by Jesus Christ (Ezekiel 36:25). In I John 2:1-2 [vs. 1] *We have an Advocate with the Father, Jesus Christ the righteous.* And also, I John 1:5-10 [vs. 9] *If we confess our sins, He is faithful and just to forgive us our sins and to cleanse us from all unrighteousness.*

Therefore to be born of the water and the Spirit is one and the same, which is a work of God, also called born again or born of God (I John 4:7-11). Have you been born again/born of God?

Thank you
Tim Barker
July 2021

About this Book

Thank you for purchasing *Ye Three Men ~ Bonus Edition*. This book is a fictitious work, and in no way is it intended to override anything contained in scripture. All things contained in this book are superseded by the Bible. After you finish this book, I strongly encourage you to read your Bible, beginning in the book of John. And please don't forget to use this book as a study guide.

There are scripture references in parentheses at the end of some sentences and paragraphs, e.g. (John 3:16). This will allow you to verify the content of that sentence or paragraph. Some places have multiple references as the sentence or paragraph was detailed. When looking up these scripture references, check to ensure you are reading the correct passage if a connection CANNOT be made. Throughout this book, quotations indicate that a character is speaking—colons (:) are utilized to indicate a long character quotation. On a few occasions, I have used curly brackets {...}. The scriptures contained within are closely associated with each other. Example: {John 3:3 & 3:5}. *Italics are utilized to indicate scripture and also when a deviation from the story is occurring.* **The bold type is used to emphasize a point.** Finally, all names utilized in this book are fictitious and are in no way implied to represent a real person.

In the back of this book are the first four chapters of:

The Cabin in the Deep Dark Woods—A Discerner of the Heart
…And…
The Cabin in the Deep Dark Woods 2—The Spirit and the Bride.

They are available on Amazon in paperback and eBook. There are a total of twenty-six chapters in each book with discussion questions and a devotional at the end of each chapter. Look for other books that I have written.

The Cabin in the Deep Dark Woods—A Discerner of the Heart.
The Cabin in the Deep Dark Woods 2—The Spirit and the Bride.
The Cabin in the Deep Dark Woods 3—Lost in the Way. Release date late 2021 or early 2022.

I have turned it into a series; however, they can be read in any order, and each book has new characters. These stories revolve around a place called Edwardsville, where there is a cabin, a mine, and a ranger station.

Also available from the author:
Ye Three Men Devotional Edition: Devotional with Scripture. In this version, the scriptures are written out in the devotional section.

Thank you for purchasing *Ye Three Men*. If you wish to be included in the newsletter, send an email to:
TheCabin@turnifyouwill.org
TheCabinInTheDeepDarkWoods.com
Thank you
Tim Barker

Ye Three Men
Chapter 1
The Price of Shoes

The sun was beginning to rise as the train rounded the last bend in the track. Waking up, the eldest man said to the other two, "We're almost to the train station." It had not been a long trip, but it got those three men where they were going. The conductor yelled, "NEXT STOP…" but that didn't matter. They had come as far as they could, spending their last dime on those train tickets. Before that, they had walked hundreds of miles on the back roads, never knowing where they were going or where they had come from. The only difference that day, they didn't have to walk while riding the train. The three men prepared to disembark, having only the clothes on their backs. Their garments were filthy long gray robes covering them down to their feet. The conductor was glad to see the likes of them gone. He said to the remaining passengers, "Someone needs to tell those three men to take a bath!" Stepping off the train onto that dirt road was the first step in their next adventure. After a while, the eldest of the three looked back, barely seeing the train station. The youngest man also looked back, then asked his two friends, "Where do we go from here?"

This is where the story begins. Those three men were walking along the way when they decided it was time they got some new shoes. The ones they were wearing had worn out long ago. The stronger man said, "Friends, my shoes are worn out." Then stopping, he said, "Look, my laces are gone, my soles have holes in them, and I've been carrying my left shoe for several miles!" He held it out, displaying its utter disrepair as if his two friends would have been surprised. The youngest man said, "My shoes aren't any better than yours." He lifted his leg displaying his foot, then wiggled his toes. Pointing to his worn-out shoe, he said, "Look, you can even see my toes wiggling." The eldest said, "We've got to keep moving, or we'll roast in this hot sun." Being in agreement, the three men continued their journey to somewhere. The eldest said under his breath, "My shoes are worse than both of yours." As they walked along the way, they saw a peculiar sign that simply said, "Shoes Ahead," with an arrow pointing them in the way to go.

As the three men traveled that new road, they passed an old woman needing assistance with her carriage. She cried out to them, saying, "Say there ye three men, I need some assistance with my carriage. It seems I've broken a wheel, and it's beyond repair. I will need a new one." Then she said, "How long have ye three men been walking in the way?" They looked puzzled by her question. She explained, "Ye three men are walking in the way of the saints of God who walked before you." (Acts 9:1-2, Matthew 3:1-3, Isaiah 40:3). The stronger man said to her: "We're sorry, but we just can't help you today. We're on our way to get some new shoes. Ours are torn, broken down, and beyond worn out." So, they left the old

Ye Three Men

woman stranded along the way. Soon after, and without any regrets, they arrived at the shoe store.

Once inside, the three men noticed how well kept the shoe store was. The shoe store clerk came from the workshop in the back of the store, smoking his corn cob pipe. The youngest of the three asked the clerk to assist them with some new shoes. "I'll be happy to help you, fellas," said the clerk. Before long, there were boxes of shoes strewn all over the store. Shortly after, each man had a box of new shoes and was ready to go. "How are ye three men going to pay me for your new shoes?" the clerk asked. "Pay you?" said the stronger man sounding surprised. "We have no money," said the eldest. Then the clerk said to them, "Well, in that case, you'll have to work for them." So, the clerk led the three men into the workshop to work off their bill. The younger man asked the clerk, "What are we going to be working on?" The clerk said: "You are going to make a new carriage wheel for an old woman who broke down along the way. She is in need and has prayed to her heavenly Father for assistance. You haven't seen her, have you? Anyway, hand me that wheel spoke over there on that workbench." The three men went to work, assisting the shoe store clerk with making the new carriage wheel. The eldest man worked on the lathe, the youngest was busy using the sander, and the stronger man glued the pieces together. After a while, the new carriage wheel was finished, and the clerk gave it to them. After handing them the new wheel, he said: "Now take this wheel to the old woman in need. You know the way. When you're finished helping her come back here and pick up your new shoes, then your bill will be paid in full."

As the men walked back to find the old woman in the way, the youngest said to his two friends, "Don't you think this trip is longer than when we traveled this road earlier?" "Yes," they both said at the same time." The elder man said, "It would have been easier if we would have helped her when we saw her in need this morning."

After a long hike in the hot sun, the three men finally arrived to help the old woman with the broken carriage wheel. Two men picked up the carriage, and the stronger man slid off the broken wheel, replacing it with the new one. After that, they said farewell to the old woman. Then she said something thought-provoking: "I saw that ye three men needed new shoes this morning, but you walked by me in such a hurry. I thought you may have seen my sign back there that said, 'Shoes Ahead.' But before I could tell you I had a carriage full of new shoes, you were off like a sprint down that road. I'm such an old woman I couldn't catch you. I just supposed that you didn't hear me. After you passed by, another traveler stopped and said, 'I need new shoes for my shoe store,' while smoking his corn cob pipe. So, I sold him all the shoes I had. I thank you so kindly for helping me today. Now I must be on my way."

Then the old woman rode off in the opposite direction that the men needed to go. The youngest man said, "Now that we're finished, we should go back. We have paid the price in full like the shoe store clerk required." They were quiet on the return trip, and they knew in their hearts that they had let down that old woman when they left her stranded earlier. They had even heard her cry for help. They didn't realize she was trying to help them with new shoes after they had refused to help her. They knew that they had only been thinking of themselves.

Once back at the shoe store, the clerk handed each man a box of shoes and asked, "What have you learned from the broken carriage wheel today, fellas?" The three men looked at one another, having nothing to say. However, with a red glow of shame, their faces said it all. Then the clerk said, "Put your new shoes on. Isn't that what you came here for?" As the three men put on their new shoes, the clerk said to them, "If you had offered to help that old woman with her broken carriage wheel this morning, she would have given you the very shoes you are wearing right now." The shoe store clerk added with a wink while taking a puff from his corn cob pipe, "Her prayer this morning went before her Father in heaven." The elder man questioned in his mind, "What could he mean, 'Her prayer this morning went before her Father in heaven?'" After that, the three men left the shoe store, having learned a valuable lesson that day. As the shoe store clerk watched those three men walk away from his store, he prayed that the Master of the Wedding Feast would take away their filthy nature by covering them with His righteousness.

Scriptures:
Acts 9:1-2, Matthew 3:1-3, Isaiah 40:3.

Ye Three Men

Chapter 2

The Wounded Man in the Way

Those three men were in such a hurry that day that they left a nice old woman to fend for herself on the side of the road. That's the old heart's way of thinking. The Lord wants to get that old nature out of those men so they are no longer self-serving. If those three men had the heart of a servant, they would not have walked past that old woman and left her stranded on the side of the road. They knew she needed help with a broken carriage wheel. God is seeking those who have a humble spirit. God wants to disclose His ways into the hearts of all people. When God writes something on the heart, it will be pure and well-pleasing in His sight. (Ezekiel 36:25-27, Psalms 51:17, II Corinthians 3:3).

The men were once again walking in the way when the eldest man said to the youngest, "I haven't seen any travelers on this road in a very long time." Soon after, the stronger man said, "Look, a traveler is coming our way." "I Don't see anyone," said the eldest. "There he is," said the youngest having better eyes than him.

Ye Three Men

"Let's befriend him," said the stronger man. The youngest replied, "How can we? We are walking towards him, and he will be suspicious when we don't pass by." The eldest man quickly turned around and started walking in the same direction as the lone traveler. Then looking back, he said to his two friends, "Turn around and walk with me!" He began walking in the way they had just come from. The two younger men didn't understand his actions, but they followed him anyway, asking his plan. "I have no plan. Only to walk slow and let him catch up to us." Then the men were walking the same way as the lone traveler who was now behind them. After a while, the lone man caught up with the three men. He introduced himself, having a burlap sack draped over his shoulder. He was wearing a working-class garment flowing to his feet. His garment, although worn, was clean and unspotted. They talked for half a day on that lonely road.

The men questioned the lone man along the way, gaining every piece of knowledge they could. He wasn't too old, and he wasn't too young. He was married with six children, two boys and four girls of various ages. His family had run into hard times during the drought that summer. The lone traveler was heading to the next village to sell his wife's jewelry and what little valuables they had left. They walked along the road for several more hours, and at dusk, the eldest man said, "We should make camp before it gets dark." They were all in agreement and camped that night at the side of the road, inviting the lone traveler to camp with them.

After they made camp, the eldest man asked the youngest, "Friend, what have you to eat tonight?" Looking puzzled, he began to speak but was quickly interrupted by the stronger man. He understood that the eldest man was attempting to swindle the loan traveler out of his rations. The stronger man said to the eldest, "Why I ran out of food just yesterday," sounding slightly downhearted. The eldest man replied, "I would have offered you my rations, but I gave them to my younger friend this morning." The loan traveler said, "I have more than enough for me and you." So he shared his rations with each of the men. They all ate very well that night.

These men were good at one time, but not any longer. They had run into hard times through no fault of their own, now they were desperate. The loan traveler slept while the elder man lay awake. He was not proud of his deceitful actions that evening. Tears formed in his eyes at the thought of swindling the loan traveler out of his rations. But they were quickly crushed by the hardness of his heart. Their hearts had become hardened through the difficulties that they had suffered in their lives. The eldest man's last thought that night was of the uncertainties that lay ahead.

Sleeping on that hard ground didn't bring much relief, but it did take the edge off, providing some rest. That night was short, and the sun began to rise before the weary travelers had found the rest they had been seeking. The youngest man was the first to awaken as the sun shown in his eyes. Rising for the day, he shouted, "Good morning," to his friends, waking the

Ye Three Men

last of the sleepers. The three men were once again walking on that lonely dusty road with their new travel companion. The village was less than half a day's travel. The men had convinced the lone traveler that they also planned to buy and sell in that village.

The lone traveler distributed the last of his food rations to his newfound friends. The four of them ate enough rations to satisfy their hunger for a few more hours. The sun was shining, and the loan traveler said to the youngest, "I thank my Lord every day that the sun rises on my family and me." The stronger man asked, "How can you thank your God when you are in the same difficulties as we?" "Faith," he replied without any hesitation, quickly picking up the stronger man's change of demeanor. The youngest asked the lone traveler, "Are you expecting a fair market return on your wife's jewelry?" The eldest knew what was happening. Soon after, the three walked to the next village to sell all they had acquired that day.

Several hours later, a Samaritan man came across the wounded man in the way. "What happened to you?" he asked, placing his hand under the lone traveler's head looking into his eyes. Unable to speak, the lone traveler just closed his eyes and faded in and out of consciousness. The Samaritan cleaned and dressed his wounds with great compassion, then placed the lone traveler on his mule. Traveling through the night, the two men made their way to the next village. Their journey was slow and difficult, arriving at the village just as the sun broke the horizon. Finding an inn, the Samaritan purchased a room for the wounded man.

After hiring someone to care for him, the Samaritan continued on his journey, promising to pay any balance when he returned.

A few days later, the wounded traveler awoke from his ordeal and told his story to the village constable. "The three men I had befriended in the way beat and robbed me of my wife's jewelry and her collection of antique brass bells. I had been traveling with all the food my family had left. And was going to sell all we owned to purchase enough food and supplies to get us through the winter months." Then the lone traveler told the constable a startling turn of events. "At first, a priest came by and poked at me with a stick. I opened my eyes but was not able to speak. He looked into my eyes, shrugged his shoulders, and said to himself, 'He must be dead because he can't answer my questions.' And walked off singing." The constable was shocked and disgusted at that man's lack of compassion for the injured. The traveler continued his story saying: "After the priest, a Levite man came by which found me naked and wounded. He was too embarrassed to assist me, saying to me, 'I'm sorry for your misfortune, but I can't possibly bring a naked and wounded man to the village. What would people think of me?' He walked off, praying in such a manner that I could hear him." The constable obtained a complete description of the priest, the Levite man, and the three thieves. He had wanted posters distributed all over town. The priest and the Levite were apprehended before sundown that day. However, the three men had escaped detection by traveling the back roads.

Ye Three Men

The constable came by the inn the next day and informed the lone traveler he had arrested the priest and the Levite, but the three men were nowhere to be found. The constable asked him, "Why did you befriend those three men traveling in the way?" The wounded traveler responded: "I was taught as a young boy that I was to love the Lord my God with all my heart, with all my soul, and with all my mind. This is the first and greatest commandment. And the second," he paused, took a drink of water, and said: "I am to love my neighbor as myself. These two commandments are essential to the Law and the Prophets. That is why I befriended those three men; they are my neighbors." (Luke 10:25-37, Matthew 22:34-40, Mark 12:28-31).

Scriptures:
Ezekiel 36:25-27, Psalms 51:17, II Corinthians 3:3, Luke 10:25-37, Matthew 22:34-40, Mark 12:28-31.

Ye Three Men

Chapter 3

An Enemy Amongst the Wheat

Several weeks had passed since robbing the lone traveler, and those three men had run out of money. Once again, they were walking in the way and met another lone traveler, but this man approached them. He was wearing a murky garment flowing to his feet, having a leather knapsack draped over his shoulder and neck. "Easy pickings," said the stronger man to himself as this new traveler joined the trio on their journey. This new traveler led all the discussions, and when he walked, he walked like an enemy. He was a step or two ahead of the other three. The stronger man asked him, "Have you any family? Are you going to the village to buy and sell? Do you have… But before he could finish his last question, the enemy shut him down coldly! He said, "Why don't you ask me another stupid question that is none of your business?!" As he said that, the stronger man noticed the enemy dipped his eyes ever so slightly. He was uncomfortable, sensing the enemy had detected the bloodstain on his garment. Soon, they came to a fork in the road, and without hesitation, the enemy chose the road to the left. The four men walked that new road for several hours before the enemy decided to camp for the night. He chose a campsite next to a hill, which no one dared to question him about.

The four men talked for hours, well into the night. Talking about this and that, never having a point about anything. That all changed instantly when the enemy spoke to the stronger man while staring at the bloodstain on his garment. He asked, "Have you any rations?" The men had planned earlier that day to save the last of their rations and befriend someone else for theirs. The stronger man sitting next to the enemy handed him half their rations. His two friends looked at him with a blank stare, wondering what had just happened. The enemy had a greater portion while the three men went hungry that night.

After finishing his rations, the enemy asked the stronger man, "Have you an education?" While the stronger man thought on that question, he noticed the enemy staring at the bloodstain of the innocent on his garment. The full moon that night shone directly on his bloodstained garment. Unable to give him a timely answer, the enemy put his hand on the stronger man's leg, making him doubly uncomfortable. Then he leaned in and whispered into the stronger man's ear, "That's why you're an imbecile." Leaving his hand on the stronger man's leg for a few moments longer, adding to his discomfort and intimidation.

The enemy boasted to the three men, "I attended university in the next village over. I have earned a degree in Inequitableness." Then he asked the elder and younger man, "Do you two gentlemen have an education?" Pausing but speaking before they could answer, "When I met you, I supposed that both of you gentlemen were highly educated." The enemy flattered them for several minutes, occasionally patting the stronger man's leg, adding to his discomfort and humiliation.

While the enemy bragged about his education and achievements, he stared at the bloodstained garment of the stronger man. This behavior made him more uncomfortable throughout the night. *This time, the stronger man began to see the loan traveler in his mind. He heard his screams for mercy. "NO! NO! NO! DON'T BEAT AND KILL ME. I HAVE A WIFE AND SIX CHILDREN!" The stronger man grabbed the lone traveler when he fell into him, imprinting the bloodstain onto his garment, then he dropped to the ground, unconscious. He had beaten him more severely than his two companions had, inflicting a severe wound to his head. They had stolen all his belongings and left him naked and wounded to die on the side of the road.*

"Now, do tell me, what kind of work do you two gentlemen attend to?" asked the enemy leaving the stronger man out of the conversation. Then he answered his own question, "I had supposed you were wealthy farmers." Looking over his shoulder, the enemy began to explain to the two men how the wheat grew on the hill behind him, giving them credit as if they were experts on the subject. He did this for some

Ye Three Men

time before turning his attention to his leather knapsack.

Opening his bag, the enemy dug out a handful of seed, saying: "I have gainfully attained employment from the wealthy plantation owner on the hill behind us. Later tonight, I will sow all this seed among the wheat. It is called darnel, and its roots grow deep into the soil, preventing erosion. The rain is coming in the morning, so this must be done tonight because the rain will wash out the wheat." Then letting the seed fall from his hand back into the bag, he closed the leather flap and leaned his bag against a rock beside where he sat. He kissed his hand and patted his bag like there was a great fortune inside. "I am so tired from all my traveling that I must get some sleep now." Then he laid down and closed his eyes for the night.

Deep in the night, while the enemy slept, the younger of the three men took the leather knapsack and woke his two friends. He whispered, "I have his bag. Let's go and distribute this seed among the wheat and receive payment from the wealthy landowner." The three men were on their way up the hill and began to sow the seed among the wheat. As they did, the enemy watched from a distance knowing in his heart what they were doing. He had deceived them into believing they were doing good when, in fact, they were actually doing evil. They had sown the tares among the wheat!

Once the three men were finished, the enemy slipped away into the night. As the sun broke the horizon, the three men approached the plantation owner, explaining they had sown the darnel among the

wheat. Then the sky opened, and the rain began to fall, mixing the darnel into the soil among the wheat. The plantation owner was in a rage and began to beat the men with his walking stick. Like a group of cowards, they ran off, knowing the enemy had deceived them into doing his evil deed. Again all three slipped out of town, walking among the back roads.
Scripture:
Matthew 13:24-30, Mark 4:26-29.

Ye Three Men

Chapter 4

The Wedding Invitation

The three men made it out of the village, escaping the wealthy plantation owner's wrath. Soon the youngest turned around and pointed in the direction they had come from. He said, "I see a horse and a rider coming our way." Shortly after, a tall man riding a magnificent white horse rode up to the three men walking in the way. Stopping, he dismounted his steed and greeted them with a royal greeting. Standing before them, the rider was wearing a snowy white garment, bright and clean, flowing to his feet with a golden bag draped around his neck and shoulder. He took off his hat and bowed before them. He said, "Dear Sirs, I am the servant of the Master of the Wedding Feast. May I join your company?" The eldest man's thoughts slipped into slow motion while he contemplated the man in white's question. Then the man became blurry, and the dirt road they had been walking on began to spin. Looking up, he saw the sun—then there were two—then four—then—then it was night.

Awakening, the eldest man found himself lying in the arms of the man in white. His head wound had been cleaned and bandaged with a torn piece of cloth from the man in white's robe. His face had been cleaned of the blood, dirt, and grass. He was drinking water from a golden cup. Having regained his composure and sitting up, the eldest man asked, "What happened to me?" The man in white said, "You passed out from your injury and lack of water." Handing him his cup, the man said, "Take another drink." Then he asked the eldest man, "How did you get that head injury?" The man in white looked at the stronger man, dropping his eyes, noticing the bloodstain on his garment. The stronger man saw his eyes and felt more uncomfortable than when the enemy did the same the night before. The eldest man explained to the man in white all that had happened with the enemy, the darnel, and the plantation owner. He explained in detail how the plantation owner struck him in the head with his walking stick and chased them down the hill where he fell, picking up the dirt and grass. Then with a slight of humor, he said, "It's a good thing he was an old man, or he would have killed us for sure." The three men felt their own degree of shame that the man in white knew their story about the tares and the wheat. However, the stronger man felt a burning degree of guilt over the lone traveler. Bitter despair was pressing upon his heart in a darkened manner. "Did my friend just confess his sins to a stranger while I hardened my heart?" thought the stronger man. The man in white said to the men, "I would be honored if you would allow me to travel this road with you." The three accepted him as a travel companion. Soon all four men were walking in the way.

As they walked, the man in white told the three men about his Master. "My Master is the greatest Man in the

Ye Three Men

land. He is the Master of the Wedding Feast and has prepared a banquet, the table is ready, the food prepared. Also, there is a wedding garment for all who will attend. I have been on a long journey inviting everyone I can to the marriage feast. Some have accepted the invitation, and others have refused. They have even injured and killed my companions. I am the only servant who remains. It is my duty to invite everyone that I come across on my journey back to my Master and His wedding." The man in white patted his golden bag, indicating that the contents were a vital part of his mission. The elder man listened intently to what the man in white had to say about the wedding feast.

Later and after numerous conversations, the youngest man said, "The day is almost gone; we will need to camp soon." The stronger man said, "Then why don't we just camp right here." Both agreed, and they stopped there and made camp for the night. The men prepared the campsite by clearing out the rocks while the man in white secured his horse. While he was gone, the stronger man said to the elder: "When you passed out this morning, you fell onto the man in white's garment like the lone traveler fell into mine, after I beat him. Yet, there is no bloodstain on his garment. What kind of a man is he?" The younger said, "We could sell his golden bag for a year's wages." The elder said, "He helped me this morning, and you want to steal from him?" The younger insisted they consider stealing the golden bag from the man in white. Then he raised his voice and said, "The golden cup is in that bag!" When he said that, the man in white had returned and heard the younger. He removed his golden bag and gestured to him that he could have it. He said, "Son, there is no need to steal. All that I have is my Master's. And all that my Master has He freely gives." The younger man refused the offer because, in his heart, he preferred to steal.

That night was unusually cold. The men had gathered wood and made a fire. As they warmed themselves, the man in white opened his golden bag and distributed his rations, saying, "Take and eat. This bread was prepared by my Master for your bodies." As the three men took the bread, the man in white gave thanks. After they had eaten the bread, the man in white opened his golden bag again. He took out his golden cup and poured wine into it, saying, "Within this cup is the testimony of my Master." He passed the cup to each of the three men. As they drank from it, he gave thanks for the wine also. The elder man tasted the sweetness in the wine, while the younger man detested the smell. Whereas the stronger man detected the bitterness in his heart. (Matthew 26:26-30, Mark 14:22-26, Luke 22:14-20).

Later that night, when the younger man was sure the man in white was sound asleep, he rose and approached him, intending to steal his golden bag. However, when he did, the elder man tripped him, causing the younger man to fall onto the man in white. This commotion woke everyone in the camp. The man in white sat up and said, "Son, if you have any need, my Master will hear you. Ask, and you will receive." Humiliated, the younger man laid back down and was silent (John 16:23-24).

After the sun rose, the three men were back on their journey. Soon coming to a fork in the road, the man in white asked his traveling companions, "Which way do you intend to go?" The stronger man spoke up and said,

Ye Three Men

"We are going to the right." The man in white removed his golden bag saying, "Then I must take the left." He handed the golden bag to the elder man, saying: "Inside are the last three wedding invitations. My Master has been expecting you and has prepared a wedding garment for each of you. Come humbled and broken, and He will not reject you." (Psalms 51:17 [NLT]). The man in white mounted his horse and rode off to the left, leaving the three men at the crossroads.

Then the man in white returned to the Master of the Wedding Feast and told Him all about the three men he found in the way. His Master asked him, **"Are they worthy to enter My wedding?"** The man in white said: "I have invited both bad and good. You will easily be able to separate them when they arrive. I warned them, just as You instructed me, that they must come humbled and broken wearing only Your righteousness."

Scriptures:
Matthew 26:26-30, Mark 14:22-26, Luke 22:14-20, John 16:23-24, Psalms 51:17.

Ye Three Men

Chapter 5

The Wedding Garment Store

After parting company with the man in white, the three men decided they needed to acquire wedding garments. Their garments were filthy, full of holes, and smelled of sweat and dirt. Several hours later, while they walked in the way, they saw a peculiar sign that simply said, "Wedding Garments Ahead." However, this time they had the golden bag of wedding invitations and a golden cup. They no longer needed to assist or rob anyone along the way. They walked the narrow path to the wedding garment store, having learned some valuable lessons from the shoe incident, the lone traveler, the enemy, and the man in white. Soon, they arrived at the wedding garment store. Once inside, they noticed several large piles of worthless garments heaped to the ceiling. The piles of discarded garments were filthy just like those they were wearing, some even worse. They observed that the discarded garments contained dried blood and smelt of human waste with a stench of urine. What a rancid smell it was

Ye Three Men

in that little store! Before long, the men learned that store was the only wedding garment store in town. The eldest man said to the younger two, "I suppose we don't have any choice. We'll have to buy our wedding garments from this store" (Revelation 3:18-22). They remembered how clean and neat the shoe store clerk kept his store and workshop. All three began to conspire how to pay for their wedding garments since they had valuables to trade.

Soon an old woman walked out from the back of the store to assist the three men. To their surprise, she was the same old woman with the shoe carriage they had abandoned in the way. "Hello again, ye three men. I remember you from the way. Now we meet again at my wedding garment store. What can I do for you?" She asked them, knowing why they were there and what they needed. And she also knew how they could obtain their wedding garments. The eldest of the three explained in great detail about the wedding invitations they received from the man in white and their ability to pay for their wedding garments. The old woman said, "Oh, I know all about the Master's wedding. I'll take good care of you boys." The stronger man lied to the old woman telling her how they had assisted other needy travelers on their journey. The younger man pointed to the golden bag and said, "We're not even concerned about the price." Then looking at the golden bag, she said to them, "Just so you know, gentlemen, you can't buy your wedding garments with anything in your golden bag."

Pointing to another room, the old woman said: "You see that room back there past the narrow gate (Matthew 7:13-14). It is in there that all of the Master's wedding garments are stored. All you have to do is enter through that narrow gate, and that's it. It's really that easy." While heading to the back of the store, she spun around and said: "Oh, just one more thing, fellas. The Master of the Wedding Feast won't let you into the wedding unless you are wearing one of the wedding garments that He has prepared for you." Then as she went to the back of the store again, the old woman's eyes caught the bloodstain on the stronger man's garment. She pointed as she asked him, "Sir, was that bloodstain there before?" "No," he answered. Gesturing to the elder man's bandaged head, he said with a nervous chuckle, "One of us was a little clumsy today." As she walked away, she said, "Liar." Then she left the three men alone.

The three men walked to the gate without any hesitation and tried to enter the wedding garment room. However, the gate was too narrow for them to fit through all at once. The youngest man said to the other two, "Let's try to enter one at a time." Then they also discovered that the gate was too narrow for them to enter single file. "What will we do?" said the stronger man to his friends. Then the eldest man reminded them, "You heard the old woman. We won't be allowed to enter the wedding feast without a wedding garment." The eldest man began to examine the narrow gate in great detail. He said, "I don't see any way for us to pass through this narrow gate on our own." Then he remembered how his heart felt when they helped the old woman with her new carriage wheel, as opposed to when they beat and abandoned the lone traveler on the side of the road to die in his nakedness.

As he was looking at the design and function of the narrow gate, the eldest man said to the other two: "Friends, this gate not only prevents us from entering the wedding garment room on our own merits but there is also a higher authority that governs its functionality." Then the eldest of the three men went outside into the street and began to cry out to the Master of the Wedding Feast. He said, "If you can hear my cry, open to me the mystery of the narrow gate!" Then he fell asleep in the middle of the street, exhausted from his travels. While he slept, he began to dream.

While dreaming, the eldest of the three men saw himself lying in the middle of the street wearing the vileness of his nature on his garment. And the bloodstains of the innocent were becoming visible. He was no longer able to hide his sins. In his dream, he saw Himself lying in a pile of manure in the mire of the street. Then as he stood and turned, the Master of the Wedding Feast stood next to him with Satan. Satan began to accuse him and point out the vileness of his nature and garment. Then the Master of the Wedding Feast rebuked that great dragon that was cast out, that serpent of old, called the devil and Satan, who deceives the whole world (Revelation 12:7-9). The eldest man clothed in his vile garment was standing alone in the mire of the street. He felt his own wickedness and corruption deep within himself, churning and emanating from his center in a virtually unexplainable manner. Then the Master of the Wedding Feast spoke to those who were witnesses and said: **"Behold I take the vileness and filth of your nature that has ravaged you and your garment. I will cause it to be removed, and I will cause a new and beautiful wedding garment to cover you and your nature. Your sin, iniquity, and immorality will pass away."** *Then the Master of the Wedding Feast warned the eldest man saying:* **"You must follow My standards and keep My commands, then you will be given responsibility over those things that belong to Me. If you continue in My ways, you may have your place with those that stand here with Me"** *(Zechariah 3:1-7).*

As the eldest man awoke out of his dream, he was still lying in the mire of the street with his face in the mud. When he stood, the mud and mire fell out of his mouth. It also fell off his garment in great clumps. Having faith that the Master of the Wedding Feast would take away all his filthiness, wickedness, and corruption, he fell to his knees. He began to shout: "I repent—I repent—I repent of my wickedness and corruption! I repent of my selfishness and idolatry! I repent of my sin of abandoning the old woman in the way, the beating of the lone traveler, and the plantation owner's field!" He did this until he was no longer able to speak, confessing one sin after another. He cried in utter brokenness with a broken spirit and a broken and a contrite heart. He cried to the Master of the Wedding Feast, "I know You will not despise my brokenness" (Psalms 51:17). Then the Spirit began to groan with words that could not be uttered or spoken (Romans 8:26). The Master is a discerner of the thoughts and intents of the heart. For the word of the Master is living and powerful, and sharper than any two-edged sword, piercing even to the division of soul and spirit, and of joints and marrow (Hebrews 4:12). The Master knows when true repentance and brokenness of the heart are occurring to save the soul. (Psalms 139:1-24, Jeremiah 17:1-13, I Corinthians 14:20-25, Ephesians 5:8-14).

He had been a sinful man, and the regrets of his heart took a while to clear out. Once he had finished repenting, he felt a peace that he could not explain. It was as if something new was on the inside, like an indwelling Spirit (II Corinthians 6:16). The best way to express this new feeling, he said, "It's the love of God" (Titus 3:5). After that, he saw that the door was still open to the wedding garment store. He ran into the store without hesitation, not even slowing down at the narrow gate, sprinting into the wedding garment room. As he did, his vile old garment was torn away at the narrow gate (Matthew 7:13-14). He could not rationalize why or how, only knowing that it was by faith and faith alone in the Master of the Wedding Feast. (Romans 1:16-17, John 3:6-8). Then falling, he rolled head over heels, making all kinds of racket falling headlong into a wedding garment rack. Then a beautiful snowy white wedding garment lay over him, covering all his nakedness, shame, and sin. His unrighteousness, iniquity, and the works of the flesh were washed away (John 3:5). When the elder man stood up, he was covered with the Master's righteousness, wearing the garment prepared for him before the foundation of the world. (Mark 9:3, Ephesians 1:4). He felt it pressed on his heart like it was being written not with ink or pen but by the hand of God (II Corinthians 3:3).

He began to walk in holiness that only comes from the Master. The elder man felt a powerful presence residing in his life and described it like God was writing an epistle on his heart and life. Suddenly a question came to his mind. *"What's the strong epistle?"* As the elder man wearing the righteousness of God thought on this, an answer came to him. He said, "The strong epistle is the one that the Master is writing on my heart." It is this strongest epistle that he will carry with him, in his heart and soul, guiding him into all truth. This strong epistle is the Holy Spirit, the Spirit of truth, the comforter, the indwelling Spirit of the living God. This will be his guide for the rest of his life. The Holy Spirit will teach him all things while he walks along the narrow path.

Scriptures:
Revelation 3:18-22, Matthew 7:13-14, Revelation 12:7-9, Zechariah 3:1-7, Psalms 51:17, Romans 8:26, Hebrews 4:12, Psalms 139:1-24, Jeremiah 17:1-13, I Corinthians 14:20-25, Ephesians 5:8-14, II Corinthians 6:16, Titus 3:5, Romans 1:16-17, John 3:5-8, Mark 9:3, Ephesians 1:4, II Corinthians 3:3, John 14.26.

Ye Three Men

Chapter 6

The Marriage Feast of the Lamb

The elder man who was wearing the wedding garment walked out of the wedding garment store. He had made quite a scene a few moments ago, both in the street and in the wedding garment room, gaining his two friends' attention. When they saw him walk outside wearing a shining wedding garment, they stopped what they were doing and met him. After that, the three men were once again walking in the way. This time they were going to the wedding feast. However, only one of them was covered with the righteousness of God. The elder man wearing the wedding garment said to his two friends, "Your garments are filthier and more disgusting than when we arrived here." He asked them, "Why is that?" The stronger man replied: "We dug through all the piles of discarded garments seeking to find garments cleaner than ours. We picked up all the filth of the flesh that was in the piles. That is why we have human waste, the stench of urine, and the matted blood of the innocent staining our garments." The elder man wearing the righteousness of God said to the two vile men, "Even those wicked sinners that killed and stole other men's wives were still given the right to repentance." (II Samuel 12:1-15, Acts 13:22). The elder man turned his head away from their foul odor. Saying: "It was in the act of repentance that those wretched sinners were able to discard their sinful nature in that wedding garment store. That's when they took on the nature of the Master, receiving the garment He prepared for them, giving them a place at His table. It is from their discarded garments that you received the blood, filth, and stench. You are still walking in the dreadful lusts of your immorality that resides in your flesh and in your nature." Then he said: "It's not just your garments that are stained, it's also your nature, and your nature has stained your garments. The blood on your hands is the blood of the innocent that you lied to, maimed, and murdered. Don't blame your sin on those who walked before you, saying we picked up their filth of the flesh by digging through a trash heap" (I John 2:16).

The elder man, with the righteousness of God emanating from his center, said: "Remember, the old woman said we won't be allowed into the wedding feast without a wedding garment. How do you suppose you will be allowed in with all your filthiness, vileness, and wretchedness?" The younger of the two walking in his own stench said: "They will not notice us. We will make it into the wedding feast on our own merits. I have my own righteousness. I don't need, nor do I want, the righteousness of the Master. I will not stoop to the lowliness and brokenness of spirit you did in your repentance that led you to receive your wedding garment from the Master" (Isaiah 64:6). The three men continued walking along the narrow path to the wedding feast. However, they walked in silence as they could no longer agree upon how to obtain the salvation of God and where to draw the line with the works of the flesh (Galatians 5:19-21).

As the three walked, they came upon a sign that simply said, "Wedding Feast Ahead." They continued their journey until they arrived at the wedding feast and went inside. The two vile men immediately sat and began to eat from the Master's table. They had not eaten lately and felt they had a right to sit, the one on the right and the other on the left (Matthew 20:20-23).

And when the King came in the assembly hall, He saw two men who were not wearing a wedding garment. He said, **"Friends, how did you come in not having a wedding garment?"** The younger man was speechless. Then with deviousness and boldness, the stronger man said, "See here, good Sir," showing the King his wedding invitation, not knowing that He was the Master of the Wedding Feast. He said to the two men, **"Did you two men read your wedding invitations?"** Both men had their invitation in hand and began to read.

> It is written: to see and enter the Kingdom of God, you must be born again. (John 3:3 & 3:5).

Then the King said to His servants: **"Bind them hand and foot, and take them away, and cast them**

into outer darkness; there shall be weeping and gnashing of teeth. For many are called, but few are chosen" (Matthew 22:11-14).

Then the Master said to the elder man wearing the wedding garment: **"I have prepared a special place for you. Come and dine with Me at My table, and I will dine with you. Set with me, and I will sit with you."** (Luke 14:7-11, Revelation 3:20).

After dining with the Master at the marriage feast, the elder man remembered his two friends who had refused to hear his testimony. Thinking as if they could still hear him: "The Master invited me to sit at his table and has spent countless hours dining with me this day. I wish you could have repented and been born again, then you would have also experienced the love of God as I have."

After the wedding feast, the elder man understood that salvation comes from Jesus Christ. He also knew when a person allows themselves to become humbled and broken, they will receive the Word of God in their heart. Then they will produce the fruit of the Spirit, which is love, joy, peace, longsuffering, gentleness, goodness, faith, meekness, temperance. Against such, there is no law.

The elder man having the love of God, said, "Those who belong to Christ have crucified the desires and lusts of the flesh." He knew that if he lived in the Spirit, he should also walk in the Spirit (Galatians 5:22-26).

The elder man walked away from the wedding feast singing, *Jesus Paid it All.* He sang that song until he arrived at his own mansion. Once inside, he said with joy and wonderment: "Oh my, I would have never imagined!"

John 14:1-2 **"Let not your heart be troubled; you believe in God, believe also in Me. "In My Father's house are many mansions; if it were not so, I would have told you. I go to prepare a place for you.**

Scriptures:
II Samuel 12:1-15, Acts 13:22, I John 2:16, Isaiah 64:6, Galatians 5:19-21, Matthew 20:20-23, {John 3:3 & 3:5}, Matthew 22:11-14, Luke 14:7-11, Revelation 3:20, Galatians 5:22-26, John 14:1-2.

Ye Three Men

Chapter 7

Every Knee Shall Bow

A man stood before the Father and read from a scroll, saying, "The Master of the Wedding Feast is the Lord Jesus Christ, and He is the Judge of the living and the dead." Then Jesus walked into the judgment hall and took His seat at the right hand of His Father and His throne. (II Timothy 4:1, Acts 10:42-43, Revelation 3:21).

Jesus said, **"Send out the next man to stand before Me in the judgment!"** The man with the scroll said, "Send out the younger man to stand before the Lord!" The younger man walked into the judgment hall and stood in the presence of the Lord Jesus Christ. Jesus asked him, **"Son, what is your name?"** Before the younger man could answer the Lord, he fell to his knees and said: "My name is Shame and Humiliation. I have stolen from the innocent, robbed the poor, and deceived the humble. I have denied the Lord Jesus Christ and blasphemed the Holy Spirit." Jesus said to His servant, **"Bring out the evidence."** The Lord's servant brought out the golden bag and opened it, and then sat the golden cup on the table of judgment. The Lord Jesus said to the younger man, **"Sitting on the table of judgment is the golden cup of the Lord that you coveted."** It was the same cup that the man in white had while on his journey. Jesus said to the younger man, **"Remember, the man in white had said to you, 'All that I have is my Master's.'"** Then Jesus said, **"Your heart is darkened and full of covetousness."** The younger man looked up and saw his Judge and the golden cup sitting on the table of judgment. He said to Jesus, "But the man in white gave me that golden cup." Jesus said to him: **"You are full of deceit, proud, unmerciful, and unforgiving. Your heart's desire was to steal the golden cup even when it was offered to you as a gift."** The Lord Jesus picked up the golden cup and gesturing to the younger man, He said, **"And if this cup had been too little, I also would have given you much more."** The younger man's judgment was set. He had been condemned to spend eternity in the lake of fire. Then the Lord's servants escorted the younger man out of the judgment hall, placed him in a holding cell, and put him in chains while the judgment continued. (Exodus 20:17, Romans 14:11, II Samuel 12:7-15, Matthew 12:31-32).

Many others stood before the Lord Jesus and were judged, condemned, and chained in the holding cell. However, every man and woman that stood before the Lord bowed the knee and said, "Jesus Christ is Lord of heaven and earth." But their confessions were too late for salvation. They had all been found guilty of denying the Lord Jesus and had also blasphemed the Spirit (Philippians 2:10-11).

Then Jesus said, **"Send out the next human to stand before Me in the judgment!"** The man with the scroll said, "Send out the stronger man to stand before the Lord!" The stronger man walked into the judgment hall and stood in the presence of the Lord Jesus Christ. Jesus asked him, **"Son, what is your name?"** Before the stronger man could answer the Lord, he also fell to his knees. He said, "My name is Thief and Liar." Jesus said to him: **"You stand before Me having your garment stained with the blood of the innocent. You have killed, maimed, and lied to My children. You have stolen the possessions of My people and squandered their belongings. A lone traveler walked beside you and spoke of My goodness and mercies, and you left him naked and wounded to die on the side of the road"** (Isaiah 55:3). Then for the first time in his life, the stronger man found himself incapable of lying while in the presence of the Lord Jesus. He said: "I have lived according to the corruption of my flesh, and I deserve to die (Romans 8:13). There is no good thing in me (Romans 7:18). I have denied the Holy One and the Just. I have killed the Prince of life, whom God raised from the dead (Acts 3:14-15). I have never repented of my sinful nature, and I have blasphemed the Holy Ghost. I am not worthy to enter the Kingdom of God." (Ezekiel 33:11, Acts 2:38, John 3:3 & 3:5). The stronger man could not believe that he had made that confession before Jesus Christ. For a split second, he questioned himself, "Why hadn't I done that before it was too late?" But that thought vanished when Jesus said to His servant, **"Bring out**

the evidence." The Lord's servant brought out the burlap sack, opened it, and sat three brass bells on the table of judgment next to the golden cup. The stronger man hadn't noticed the table of judgment until the Lord Jesus allowed him to stand and face the evidence. After that, the blood of the innocent began to drip from the stronger man's filthy garment. Jesus said, **"The blood of the innocent cries out to Me from the ground."** (Psalms 10:8-11, Genesis 4:10).

Before the Lord Jesus cast His judgment on the stronger man, Jesus walked over to the table of judgment and picked up one of the brass bells. He rang the bell only once and said: **"A couple of years after you stole these brass bells from the lone traveler, they ended up in a shoe store. It was the shoe store clerk with the corn cob pipe who picked up this brass bell and rang it once, starting a worship service that sparked a revival lasting for centuries that was called the Great Revival of the Glory of God. During that revival, millions upon millions of people cast off their bloodstained garments becoming born again in that little wedding garment store on the narrow path."** Then Jesus looked at the stronger man, whose name was Thief and Lier, and said to him, **"What you intended for evil, I intended for good."**

The stronger man's judgment was also set, he had been condemned to spend eternity in the lake of fire, but he was given a greater judgment. (Isaiah 14:19, Luke 17:1-4, Revelation 21:8). Then the Lord's servants escorted the stronger man out of the judgment hall and placed him in the holding cell in chains along with the others. Then a lever was thrown, sending that holding cell train they were on to their torments into the lake that burns with fire and brimstone. As that train rounded the last bend in the track, their screams filled the judgment hall. It had not been a long trip, but it got those people where they were going. The conductor yelled, "NEXT STOP..." but that didn't matter. They had come as far as they could.

Scriptures:
II Timothy 4:1, Acts 10:42-43, Revelation 3:21, Exodus 20:17, Romans 14:11, II Samuel 12:7-15, Matthew 12:31-32, Philippians 2:10-11, Isaiah 55:3, Romans 8:13, Romans 7:18, Acts 3:14-15, Ezekiel 33:11, Acts 2:38, {John 3:3 & 3:5}, Psalms 10:8-11, Genesis 4:10, Isaiah 14:19, Luke 17:1-4, Revelation 21:8.

The End ~ Ye Three Men.

Also available: ***Ye Three Men Devotional Edition: Devotional with Scripture.*** In this version, I have added a devotional section where the scriptures are written out in the devotionals. This book is available on Amazon.com

THE CABIN IN THE DEEP DARK WOODS

A Discerner of the Heart

(the first four chapters only)

Tim Barker

The Cabin in the Deep Dark Woods ~ The first four chapters only.
Published by Tim Barker
Published in New Port Richey, FL 34654, U.S.A.

All scripture is taken from the New King James Version® unless otherwise noted. Copyright © 1982 by Thomas Nelson. Used by permission. All rights reserved.

Scripture quotations marked [AMP] are taken from the AMPLIFIED Bible, Copyright © 1954, 1958, 1962, 1964, 1965, 1987, 2015 by The Lockman Foundation. All rights reserved. Used by permission. (www.Lockman.org)

Scripture quotations marked [NLT] are taken from the Holy Bible, New Living Translation, copyright © 1996, 2004, 2007, 2013. Used by permission of Tyndale House Publishers, Inc., Carol Stream, Illinois 60188. All rights reserved.

Scripture quotations marked [KJV] are from the King James Version of the Bible.
ISBN 978-1-951615-00-0
Library of Congress Control Number: 2020911666
Copyright © 2020 By Timothy L. Barker
Cover Design at date of publication: Tim Barker
Editor: Bonnie Olsen

The Cabin in the Deep Dark Woods ~ the first four chapters only

Chapter 1 ~ Friday
The Journey Begins

I want to tell you a story about a group of kids whose lives were changed many years ago while visiting a cabin one weekend in late autumn. This trip started out on a typical Friday morning and promised to give everyone some hiking, some exploring, and some well-needed relaxation. However, what occurred on that trip was nothing short of an adventure. This is the account of how it all transpired.

As the group was hiking along the first marked trail making their way to the cabin, two of the boys fell behind the others. As Peter Myers and Mark Phillips talked to each other, they became captivated by the scenery and the beauty of nature all around them. They saw the hills and the valleys with the mountain peaks in the background. Suddenly, there was a man wearing a hooded cloak with his face concealed that looked very similar to a hooded man from a gas station earlier that same day. He began following them, having his face veiled. Realizing that they had fallen behind the others, the two boys decided to take a short cut along an unmarked trail. There they were met by another man, wearing a hooded cloak with his face also veiled. The first hooded man called them by name, saying, "Eyes sees you, eyes sees you, Peter Myers. Eyes sees you, eyes sees you, Mark Phillips. Come to me, and I will give you a treasure that will enlighten you and your friends." Peter and Mark started to walk back the way they had come, but the second hooded man blocked their way. Mark yelled to Peter, "RUN!" As both boys begin to run further and further into the deep dark woods down the unmarked trail, fear began to grip their very being. There is a type of fear that prevents a person from screaming for help, and it is terrifying. This type of fear gripped both boys. Peter and Mark were caught in between those two hooded men and were trying to escape.

Clark Williams, one of the youth leaders, felt the need to do an on the march headcount as he sensed that something was wrong. He counted, again and again, not letting anyone else know that he had been short on the headcount twice or perhaps even five times. With a slight panic in his voice, Clark yelled, "WHO'S MISSING?! WHO IS MISSING?!" Brenda Summers looked around and said, "It's Peter and Mark!" And at once, everyone stopped and began to yell for them. Jill Williams, Clark's wife and co-leader, was thinking to herself, "This can't be happening, this just can't be happening!" "PETER, MARK, WHERE ARE YOU TWO?!" Everyone yelled in unison, without an answer as to their whereabouts.

Eight Hours Earlier at Peter Myers's Home

It was early Friday morning, and Senior Pastor James Myers began to prepare his Sunday morning message as he had done every week for the past seven years. He had been following an outline on the Holy Spirit and was nearly three-quarters of the way through it. He thought that he was ready for something else to preach on. He said to himself, "I'm not sure if I want to preach on the Holy

The Cabin in the Deep Dark Woods

Spirit anymore. I'm just not feeling it." Afterward, he caught himself looking around his study, peering down the hallway and thinking to himself, "I hope I didn't say that out loud! No one wants a pastor who is burnt out preaching on the Holy Spirit and a senior pastor at that." Then he said out loud, "Of course, no one wants to hear that." Peter thought he heard his dad and yelled from the other room, "Did you say something, Dad?" Pastor James answered, "No, I was just talking to myself, never mind me." Then Pastor James said to himself, "Okay, James, you have to keep all that burn out stuff to yourself, buddy, there are no other jobs out there for you. Nobody wants to hire an old charred pastor." "Hey, Dad, I'm going to load my gear into the truck. Can we leave soon? Oh, and remember you said that you would take me to get a sandwich on the way to the church," Peter said.

At that, Pastor James broke his pencil. He mumbled something under his breath as he yelled back across the house, "I'll be just a few more minutes to finish this thought," as several of his church problems were raging through his mind. "Okay, no problem, just remember the church van leaves at 10:00 a.m. sharp." Peter reminded his dad, not knowing that it was beginning to irritate him. "Got it," said Pastor James with a cynical undertone that only he caught. "Hey, Dad," Peter said, once again yelling across the house, "did I tell you that Mark was coming over, and we are giving him a ride to the church?" Once again, Pastor James held in his emotions with a slightly cynical undertone by saying to his son, "No problem, Peter." And while throwing his arms up in the air, he added under his breath, "I've got all day to get this sermon ready for the Sunday morning service. I can run kids all over town, no problem. I just hope my congregation appreciates all that I do for this church."

Mark Phillips and his grandmother arrived at the Myers's home. Peter ran outside and gave his best friend a high five and then helped him load his camping gear into the truck. Mark said to Peter, "This trip is going to be so good. I've been looking forward to it for a long time." They made their way into the house after the last of the camping gear was stowed away in the truck.

Pastor James was speaking with Mark's grandmother, Gertrude Phillips, in the kitchen. "Good morning Mrs. Phillips," he said, "here's my phone number if there is anything you need while Mark is away on his trip," handing her his business card. "Why thank you, Pastor, I really appreciate this," said Mrs. Phillips. She said that while holding his business card up to the light and staring at it. "Gertrude. Gertrude! Mrs. Phillips?!" Pastor James finally gained the attention of Mark's grandmother. He said, "Ma'am, I can assure you that it's my business card." Mrs. Phillips quickly took it down and put it in her coat pocket. "Oh dear, oh dear, I'm so sorry, I couldn't see it clearly," she said, acting a little confused.

It was during that time Peter and Mark entered the kitchen. Mark remembered that his grandmother had not been acting herself lately. Peter gave Mark a look as if to say, is everything alright with your grandmother? Just then, Stacy Myers entered the room, not knowing what had transpired a moment ago and said, "Hey dear, don't you think it's time you get these two young lads on the road, so they can get to the church?" Pastor James answered, "I'm sorry, Mrs. Phillips, I will need to be going." As he walked away, he rolled his eyes at his wife.

The Cabin in the Deep Dark Woods

Not looking at the two boys, Pastor James headed to the truck saying in a slight huff, "Let's get this show on the road." He was still questioning his wife's logic that he had time to take the boys to the church.

Jill Williams had gotten up bright and early to get the final odds and ends packed for the retreat that weekend. She made sure that she and her husband Clark had the reservation paperwork for the cabin packed in one of their bags, which was the responsibility of the youth group leaders. "Clark, you need to get up. We should be leaving in the next few minutes. Clark! CLARK! Did you hear me? Clark, would you please get up now?!" Jill said sternly as her frustration and anxiety were making their way to the surface. Clark rolled out of bed and headed to the kitchen. He asked her, "Jill, did you make coffee this morning?" "NO, and you don't have time to either," she answered. Then she asked, "Did you pack your backpack yet?" Clark responded to his wife's question by gesturing with his backpack holding it up, indicating that it was packed and ready to go. Clark said, "By the way, I filled the gas tank, got the oil changed, and had the tires rotated on the church van so we can leave the church as soon as all the kids are loaded up." Jill gave him a look that said, I can't believe you made coffee. Then she said, "There wasn't enough time, you should have gotten up an hour ago." Clark grabbed his backpack and coffee mug, thinking that she's the one that should have made it in the first place. He walked past his wife, picked up her bag, and asked her, "Is your bag ready?" He headed to the car with Jill following, and she locked the door behind them.

On the way to the church, Pastor James stopped at the Old Horse Thief Hamburger Stand to get a burger for himself and the boys. While standing in line, Mark asked Peter in a whisper, "Is your dad alright? He doesn't seem to be himself lately. I mean, he's different at church. Is everything okay at home?" "What will you boys be ordering today?" asked the cashier. Peter used that moment to evade the question from Mark, ignoring his best friend. Pastor James said to her, "Three hamburgers, three orders of french fries, and three sodas—oh and to go." He didn't even stop to consider that the boys may want to order something different. After all, they were high school students, not little children anymore. Pastor James was quiet while the order was prepared. Mark took advantage of that time to reiterate the question. He looked into his best friend's eyes, asking the question once more, sensing that something was just not right about Peter's dad. "Yeah, he's been a little bit cranky and irritable lately, that's for sure. I'm definitely ready for this trip," said Peter, seeming a little embarrassed having said that about his dad. "Order number 430. Sir, is your ticket 430?" asked the cashier. "Oh yes," said Pastor James. He paid for the order and headed to the door, not looking back to see if the two boys were coming with him. "Hey, we better go, your dads leaving without us," Mark said, grabbing Peter's arm and heading for the door.

Pastor James was driving to the Truth Valley Church while the radio played on 91.5 the ROCK FM. "Hey, everyone out there in radio land," said the D.J., Rex Redman, loudly. Pastor James turned the volume down a bit. "I'm glad you're all here listening to the ROCK FM. I've got a special guest speaker today, Pastor Melvin Baldwin, from Southland Bible College," said Rex, introducing him. Pastor Baldwin began his message by

The Cabin in the Deep Dark Woods

saying: "Thank you, Rex, I always love being a part of the ROCK FM. Today I'm going to speak to you from Matthew 7:21-23. In this passage, we find there will be some people, even members of local churches, that will one day stand before Jesus Christ and have those horrible words spoken to them, 'depart from Me.' It was clear that Jesus was speaking to people who thought they were saved but were never truly converted. Who may these people be…" "CLICK" went the radio dial as Pastor James turned it off. Just then, Mark looked over at Peter, both boys wondered why Peter's dad turned the radio off since the guest speaker was just getting started with his message. Mark thought to himself, "Could I be one of those people?"

It was pretty quiet the rest of the way, and all three were consumed with eating their meal as Pastor James made his way to the church. However, Mark couldn't shake that question as it continued to play in his mind, "Who may these people be…?"

The Cabin in the Deep Dark Woods ~ the first four chapters only

Chapter 2 ~ Friday
That Treasure Chest

Soon Pastor James arrived at the Truth Valley Church with Peter and Mark, and the others were arriving. The three Summers sisters, Brenda, Daisy, and Lisa, the youngest and their brother Brad were dropped off by their mother, Sara. She also gave Brenda's best friend, Becky Owens a ride. Andrew Jeremiah was the last of the kids to arrive at the church. Soon after, Mr. and Mrs. Williams, the youth leaders for that year's trip to the Cabin in the Deep Dark Woods, also arrived at the church. All the campers had loaded their camping gear into the van and were ready to go. Before they left, Peter said to Mark, "Hey, I'm sorry about how my dad's been acting; he's just not been himself lately."

"You all have fun on your trip and drive safely," Pastor James yelled as Clark was pulling the van out of the church parking lot. The sign on the back of the van said, "OFF TO THE CABIN WE GGGOOOOOOOO!!" Clark looked over at his wife and said, "This is going to be an eye-opening trip for everyone." "You had better believe it," she replied. They could hear the kids in the back of the van singing out the church's motto, "Where the truth of the Spirit flows into the valley."

The Cabin in the Deep Dark Woods

Soon the group made their first stop for gas on their six-hour drive to the cabin. Before anyone exited the van, Clark said to the group, "Be sure to use the buddy system." Peter and Mark teamed up and went around to the back of the gas station, where there was a scenic view from the mountain they were on. As the two boys went around the corner, they bumped into a man wearing a hooded cloak with his face concealed by a veil. He was walking in the other direction, toward the front of the gas station. Thinking no more about him, they viewed the other mountains that were all around them. The sun was illuminating all the beauty before their eyes. Soon they decided they should be heading back to the van. "All in, we're ready to rock and roll," Jill said, as the headcount was right on the money. She added with emphases, "We don't want to lose any of these children the Lord has given us" (Hebrews 2:10-18).

It was a few hours later when the church van pulled into the parking lot of the Cabin in the Way. Before anyone got out, Clark said to the kids, "Don't forget your gear, and above all else, remember, stay together." The long trek to the cabin was about to begin along the first marked trail. That cabin had been used by the Truth Valley Church for many years; it had even become a generational event. There were some kids on that trip whose parents had been to the cabin when they were young. **It's known as the Cabin in the Deep Dark Woods; that's what they called it at Truth Valley. It's really called the Cabin in the Way, a part of a larger property that belongs to the state**

parks department. It was at this cabin that our story took place. I am about to tell you how a group of kids and their youth leader's lives were changed while visiting the Cabin in the Way on a much-needed retreat from everyday life. This trip started out on a typical Friday morning that promised to give everyone a bit of hiking, some exploring, and some well-needed rest. However, what occurred there was nothing short of an adventure. **This is how it all began as we rejoin our campers on their hike to the Cabin in the Deep Dark Woods.**

The main group of hikers was now in full panic mode and desperately searching for Peter and Mark. Clark was walking around in circles with his hands on his head, wondering how this situation could have happened. He heard his wife's voice piercing into that part of his brain that was controlling his panic. "Clark, you can't just stand there and think that you are going to find Peter and Mark like that, you have to do something, anything!" Jill said. Brad jumped into the conversation and said, "Mr. Williams, we could walk back the way we came and…" "That's perfect," Jill interrupted him, as she began leading the group back the way that they had come while pulling Clark along by his arm.

Once again, Peter and Mark found themselves running the other way to escape the two hooded men. Panic was flowing through their veins like ice water down a mountain stream in the springtime. Peter tripped over an old cypress stump, and Mark started to run back the way they came. Mark looked back, seeing

The Cabin in the Deep Dark Woods

Peter lying on the ground and knowing in his heart that he couldn't leave his best friend to face them alone. Mark turned around and ran back. After he grabbed Peter by the arm and helped him up, one of those hooded men stood in front of them, and the other was standing behind them.

The first hooded man once again said to the boys, "Eyes sees you, eyes sees you, Peter Myers. Eyes sees you, eyes sees you, Mark Philips. Come to me, and I will give you a treasure that will enlighten you and your friends." Peter and Mark looked at one another, not knowing how they could escape at that point. The first hooded man said, "Behold, I stand at the door and knock" (Revelation 3:20). Then he handed a treasure chest to Peter and said, "Remember to use the filter, it will be most helpful to you and your friends." Then the hooded men disappeared into the deep dark woods. Peter and Mark quickly made their way out of the short cut and caught up to the main group. Peter had buried the treasure chest deep within his backpack to hide it from the others.

"Hey, where were you two? We were just searching for you," Andrew said. "Welcome back, boys," Clark said, as he felt relieved by their safe return, and at the same time, his despair was vanishing away. "Now, let's get on with our hike before it gets dark." Clark made an emphasis on the fact that they had to make it to the cabin before sunset. As they walked along the first marked trail, a set of glowing eyes followed them, but no one noticed.

The group finally made their way to the cabin just as the sun was going down. The last light of day was vanishing, and a beautiful sunset was leaving its mark in the sky. "Well, that was close," Brad said as they all got into the cabin just before dark. Peter and Mark went back outside and were sitting on the stone wall in front of the cabin. Peter was still a little shaken-up by the encounter with the man wearing the hooded cloak. He said to Mark while he pulled the treasure chest out of his backpack, "What do you think about this treasure chest that dude gave me?" "I don't know, man," Mark replied, I would be afraid to open it tonight; let's just put it under your bed and forget about it. Maybe we can just leave it here in the cabin. Just don't tell anybody about what happened back there in the woods, nobody will believe us anyway." Peter replied, "That's for sure."

Once back inside the cabin, Peter and Mark saw Andrew, and he asked them, "Hey, where did you two guys get that treasure chest?" They tried to hide it, but Jill also saw it and said, "Wow, Peter, that's a beautiful treasure chest you have there." Turning around to look, Brad bumped into Peter's arm, causing him to drop the treasure chest on the hardwood floor. Then a brand-new state of the art video camera fell out. "Wow," said Brad, "where did you guys get that video camera? It must have cost a bazillion dollars; that thing is way cool!" Clark saw all the commotion and also the new video camera lying on the floor. "Peter," he asked, "where did you get that video camera? I don't remember you having it earlier today." Peter said, "It's a long story." "Yeah," said Mark interrupting, "it's a long story, and we're getting pretty tired, so maybe we can tell you all about it tomorrow." At that, the group began the process of retiring for the night.

Jill said, "It's going to be a big day tomorrow," referring to the annual hike to the Edwardsville Ranger Station. Jill was leading all the girls to their side of the cabin. She said, "We'll see you fellas in the morning, and don't forget to make breakfast." She was rubbing in the fact that the girls raised more money for that trip than the boys did—hence the loser of the wager had to cook breakfast for the entire retreat. Jill said, "Goodnight, all you egg heads. Don't forget to get cracking bright and early for our breakfast. I like mine over easy." The rest of the night was uneventful as everyone was tired. It had been a long day getting everything ready for the trip and then that twenty-minute hike to the cabin. All was quiet outside as the crickets played a tune that matched the tranquility of the wilderness view of the mountain range. There were, however, some men wearing hooded cloaks with eyes aglow watching over the cabin and those within.

The Cabin in the Deep Dark Woods ~ the first four chapters only

Chapter 3 ~ Saturday An Ancient Scroll

Beep—Beep—Beep. "WOULD YOU TURN THAT THING OFF AND MAKE MY BREAKFAST!" Jill said to Clark. She wasn't a big fan of her husband's alarm clock, especially when he slept through it. Jill could hear her husband murmuring under his breath about her comment. She was thinking about how things in their marriage weren't as good as most people thought. She put on her happy face and roused all the girls suggesting they get to the bathroom before the boys got up.

Breakfast went as planned, and clean up went fast as the girls pitched in so the day's activities could begin. "I'm so excited," Becky said, as she tucked her Bible under her arm. She sat at the kitchen table for that morning's devotional session, which Andrew led. Andrew held regular Bible studies at his public high school and had prepared a few lessons for that trip. Andrew started the lesson by saying, "Today's Bible lesson is from Hebrews 11:6, which says that without faith, it is impossible to please God." Andrew continued with his lesson, and all the kids felt they got something out of it. Though some thought he took the Bible too seriously for a high school kid. Some also wondered if he had intentions of being a pastor. His teachings seemed to have more substance than their own Senior Pastor's did at

The Cabin in the Deep Dark Woods

times. Becky and Lisa were the first ones to leave the table, even before Andrew had a chance to end his lesson. Becky said to Lisa, "I just hate it when he talks about all that faith crap, I got enough faith anyway!"

After that lesson by Andrew, the youth group had planned to take a hike along the second marked trail, over the red covered bridge, down to the ranger station. Every year the Truth Valley Church youth group would take a tour of the ranger station and the abandoned Edwardsville Mine and Millworks Company. It was this field trip that everyone had been looking forward to. Then Clark got everyone's attention and said, "We're going to start the day with our hike to the ranger station. Get your partners and team up, and remember, stay together!" He said that looking directly at Peter and Mark.

Peter and Mark had been best friends since grade school and were on the same little league baseball team for five years straight. Brenda always said about Peter and Mark, "You would think those two were brothers; you just can't separate them," she was the oldest of the Summers children. The Summers family lost their father Ricky from an illness and have struggled since. Soon after, they lost their house and were forced to get a government-subsidized apartment. Their mother Sara worked a lot of nights and missed church more often than not. Some even said she was a backslider, now that her husband was gone. But they always ended with, "bless her little heart for trying so hard." Well, that's the talk of the church at the Coffee Barn, where the gossip goes down, and the truth is never found.

The three older Summers children became aware of God when things were good at home, before their father got sick. On the other hand, Lisa became aware of God when her father, Ricky first became ill. The three older children had been grounded in God. They had a foundation, where Lisa, the youngest, never received that needed parental attention, and she fell by the wayside. She never received the foundation to develop a belief in God. As the months and years flew by, during Ricky's illness, Lisa became hardened by all the stress and the general lifestyle of the Summers's household. Sara prayed daily for God to heal her husband. It was just over two years since Ricky started feeling bad until he passed away, and Lisa got lost in all that mess.

Once all the students had their hiking partners, they were off to the ranger station. As the group was hiking along the second marked trail, Clark pointed out some trees and some different kinds of foliage. There were some markers with a short description of the native species. "Look over there," Brad said, as he pointed out some wildlife down by the creek. The hike was uneventful as the group made their way to the ranger station, where they could officially check-in and turn in the reservation paperwork.

Halfway through the hike, Peter and Mark once again fell behind the others before anyone had a chance to make it to the red covered bridge. Suddenly, another hooded man appeared out of nowhere and said to them, "Eyes sees you, Peter Myers, and eyes sees you, Mark Phillips." They tried to run away from the hooded man, but another one came from behind and put a clay jar in Peter's hands. The first one said to Peter and Mark, "If anyone hears My voice and opens the door." Then the hooded man disappeared into the deep dark woods just as the second

The Cabin in the Deep Dark Woods

one walked back the way he came. Peter and Mark decided they needed to stay with the group because these hooded men were beginning to freak them out.

After a few minutes, they caught up to the group. Daisy asked, "Hey guys, what's in the clay jar?" She grabbed for it, causing it to open, dropping its contents on the ground in front of everyone. Andrew said, "Hey, that looks like an ancient scroll." Clark asked, "Where did you two boys get that?" Mark told him that they found it. He said that because he thought the truth would be too hard to explain. "Is that true, Peter?" asked Jill. "Well, yeah, kind of," said Peter. "Kind of?" asked Clark. Then he said, "First, a video camera falls out of a treasure chest, and now an ancient scroll falls out of a clay jar. What's going on, you two?" Peter said, "I'm just not sure?" Jill interrupted them, saying, "We should be heading back to the cabin now. I've noticed the clouds are starting to build to the north. I think a storm is coming our way." At that, the group headed quietly back to the Cabin in the Way. They were not able to make it to the ranger station that day. Everyone made it safely inside the cabin just as the first raindrop fell, and a thunderclap shouted a warning that this storm was going to be a fierce one.

Once inside, Jill and Clark started to get lunch ready while the kids put away their backpacks from the morning hike. After a few minutes of preparation, lunch was served. Jill rang the cowbell telling everyone to come and get it. Peter and Mark were still sitting on their beds and looking at the scroll while the others started eating their lunch.

"Hey, Peter, what does it say on the scroll?" Mark asked. Peter looked hard at the scroll and read the markings out loud, "It says Revelation 3:20." Mark asked, "Was that there before?" Peter replied, "No, I'm sure it wasn't. Grab that Bible, and let's look it up." Mark grabbed a Bible that was lying on the table, in-between the rows of beds, and read aloud. "Behold, I stand at the door and knock. If anyone hears My voice and opens the door, I will come into him and dine with him, and he with Me." "Whoa, whoa, whoa, stop right there, that's the same thing the hooded man said to us in the woods," Peter shouted. With that, he got the attention of the others who were eating lunch at the table, and they looked over at Peter and Mark. "Hey, that's my mom's Bible," Lisa said. "What do you mean, that's Mom's Bible. Our father gave that to her; you just can't take it on a camping trip!" Daisy said. Just then, Brad jumped up and grabbed the ancient scroll out of Peter's hand and said to Peter and Mark, "That wasn't written there before." He picked up his mother's Bible and read the scripture aloud for everyone to hear. Then Brad asked, "Mr. Williams, what does this scripture mean?" Clark looked at the group of teenagers, and the only thing that he knew about this verse was superficial at best, so he gave it a shot. He said, "Well, guys, this scripture, this verse, this passage in the Bible was written by the Apostle John to get our attention so that we can serve Jesus better. Yep… that's right, it was written so we can serve Him better." Clark thought he nailed that one. Then his head popped when Andrew said, "Uh, Mr. Williams, with all due respect." He reached for the open Bible of Mrs. Summers that was now laying on Mark's bed.

    Andrew continued by saying: "This scripture is all about our Lord and Savior Jesus Christ

The Cabin in the Deep Dark Woods

being outside His church because the people inside want to do church their way. When the will of the Father (John 6:39-40) is not followed, Jesus is the one outside. When the scriptures are not followed, Jesus is the one outside; when prayer is dead, Jesus is outside. The only way to get Jesus back in the church is through true repentance and brokenness of the heart and spirit."

Jill said, looking directly at her husband, "Well, I guess someone hasn't been reading his Bible. Thank you, Andrew Jeremiah, for that interpretation." No one except Peter, Mark, and Brad noticed the scroll had Revelation 3:20 written on it. Brad looked hard at the two boys and said, "You better come clean and tell me what's going on here. Where did this Ancient scroll come from?!" So, Peter let Brad in on everything that happened on the trail with the hooded men, the video camera, and the ancient scroll. Brad said, "You two are starting to freak me out. So, let me get this straight, you two were on the trail when you encountered a…"

Just then, Brenda yelled, "HEY, PETER! Get your video camera; the storm is really getting bad! I see a tornado!" As Peter grabbed the video camera, he fumbled around while trying to turn it on, but he couldn't find the power button. Then suddenly, it came on by itself and began to film Brenda. As Peter watched through the video screen, it was extremely blurry, with two shadows on either side of her. "I can't see anything," Peter said to Mark. **Just then, Mark remembered the words of the first hooded man from the woods, "Remember to use the filter; it will be most helpful to you and your**

friends." Mark reminded Peter about the filter and the words of the hooded man. Then Peter found the filter dial and turned it all the way to the right. As Peter looked up from the camera video screen, he couldn't believe what he saw outside; the storm lifted away, the tornado vanished, and the sun came out just like a brand-new day. Peter was again fixed on the camera's screen. Then Brenda and her two sisters became visible after he adjusted the filter dial. Peter motioned for Brad to look at the camera screen with him. Jill came around to watch and said, "Turn up the volume," then the volume turned up on its own. Brenda, Daisy, and Lisa were all clearly visible on the camera view screen. A voice began to speak, saying, "The kingdom of heaven is like ten young virgins."

The Cabin in the Deep Dark Woods ~ the first four chapters only

Chapter 4 ~ Saturday
The Wise Took Oil

The camera displayed all on its own all three of the Summers sisters on the video screen. Then the voice of an angel was heard narrating what the three girls were doing. The camera continued to play out the scene of the young virgins.

All three Summers sisters were seen on the viewscreen as if they were in a movie. The video camera viewed them from the perspective of God, how that they were actually known by Jesus, and the Holy Spirit revealed who they really were spiritually.

The kingdom of heaven is like ten young virgins, which took their lamps and went out to meet the Bridegroom. Five of them were wise, among them were Brenda and Daisy. And five were foolish, among them was Lisa. The foolish ones took their lamps and brought no oil with them, but the wise took oil in their containers with their lamps. While the Bridegroom was delayed, they all slept. At midnight there was a cry made, "Behold, the Bridegroom comes, go out to meet Him." Then all the virgins arose and made their lamps ready. The foolish virgins said to the wise, "Please give us some of your oil, for our lamps are gone out." But the wise answered, saying, "No, there won't be enough for us and you, go to them who sell, and buy for yourselves." While they went to buy, the Bridegroom came. And those who were ready went in with Him to the wedding, and the door was shut. Afterward, the foolish virgins came, saying, "Lord, open to us." But he answered and said, "I can assure you, I don't know you." Watch and be alert, for you do not know the day nor the hour when the Son of Man is coming (Matthew 25:1-13).

The three Summers sisters were watching in shock and horror as Lisa was given the verdict that she was one of the foolish virgins, which the Bridegroom did not know.

And the smoke of her torment ascends forever and ever. She will have no rest day or night (Revelation 14:11). At this point, everyone in the group was watching, and they saw Lisa being cast into the Lake of Fire on the video screen. She was wholly engulfed in the flame of the fire that burns forever and ever. Lisa was heard belting out screams that did not sound human in origin. Just before the camera screen went blank, Lisa was heard utterly despising God with blasphemies that were directed towards Him and His nature. Shouting out words so hideous, no one could imagine that a human could be so depraved. Having no hope of escaping her torments, her entire being hated God. Knowing instantly, the lake of fire was her new home, her eternal residence, and that the fire would never cease to torment her day and night, year after year, century after century, endlessly. Then the video camera shut off, and the screams of Lisa seemed to linger in the cabin for a few moments longer.

The Summers children gathered around Lisa and consoled her as the video was very graphic. It depicted that she had not been born again when the Lord Jesus came calling. Brenda looked at her sister Daisy and asked,

"Could it be possible that Lisa has never been born again?" Daisy looked at Lisa, who was now sitting on the cabin floor, and asked her, "Lisa, have you ever accepted Jesus Christ as your personal savior?" Lisa looked up and said in a humble mannerism, "I don't know, maybe not. I said a prayer once, or maybe even twice, I'm not sure anymore. I just don't understand how to be saved." Then with tears flowing, Lisa began to weep and cry out, displaying utter brokenness as she called upon the name of the Lord Jesus.

Lisa said, "Lord, I have never given You place in my life, and I want to change that right now. I want You to be my Savior and my Lord." Lisa began to confess her sins to Jesus Christ. Those in the cabin felt the brokenness of her spirit. This went on for quite some time with lots of tears. Then after that, Lisa fell into the arms of her siblings, saying there was a peace that had come over her that she could not describe in words. It was the very opposite of what had been expressed in the video. Then the camera turned back on by itself, and Brad was seen by all on the camera screen.

The End ~ The Cabin in the Deep Dark Woods ~ A Discerner of the Heart—the first four chapters only.

The full 26 chapter novel, *The Cabin in the Deep Dark Woods ~ A Discerner of the Heart*—is available on Amazon.com

Book Overview:

There is a place where Jesus discerns the thoughts and intents of the heart. Join this group of high school students as they embark on an adventure while visiting the Cabin in the Deep Dark Woods. They will find themselves engrossed in a story as Jesus reveals who they are. Some will be challenged when they find out their eternal destiny is in jeopardy. There will be some exciting and tense moments during this adventure as their hearts are exposed at the Cabin in the Way. Who will be able to overcome the truth within? Will a time of repentance be instilled in the hearts of this group? Can they find a way to bring home the life-altering events that unfold? Join Peter, Mark, Brenda, Becky, and the rest of the gang as they discover the profound truth of their hearts as revealed by Jesus. Are you brave enough to join them? If so, follow along by participating in the discussion questions and the devotional at the end of each chapter.

The Cabin in the Deep Dark Woods 2
The Spirit and the Bride
(the first four chapters only)

Tim Barker

Tim Barker

The Cabin in the Deep Dark Woods 2 ~ The first four chapters only.
Published by Tim Barker
Published in New Port Richey, FL 34654, U.S.A.

All scripture is taken from the New King James Version® unless otherwise noted. Copyright © 1982 by Thomas Nelson. Used by permission. All rights reserved.

Scripture quotations marked [NLT] are taken from the Holy Bible, New Living Translation, copyright © 1996, 2004, 2007, 2013. Used by permission of Tyndale House Publishers, Inc., Carol Stream, Illinois 60188. All rights reserved.

Scripture quotations marked [KJV] are from the King James Version of the Bible.
ISBN 978-1-951615-02-4
Library of Congress Control Number: 2021905574
Copyright © 2021 By Timothy L. Barker
Cover Design at date of publication: Tim Barker
Editor: Bonnie Olsen

The Cabin in the Deep Dark Woods 2 ~ the first four chapters only

Chapter 1 ~ Saturday
On a Hill Far Away

Marcus looked into the man's eyes and said to him, "You have to get up now; it's just a little further." The man continued to struggle with the weight of his burden. At that moment, Marcus realized the prisoner wasn't going to make it up the hill on his own. He was resting on one knee and trembling while the sweat dripped from his brow. Then the prisoner looked Marcus in the eyes, piercing his soul. "Who are you?" Marcus asked him in a whisper.

Frozen in thought for a moment, Marcus felt the sweat fall from his own brow. Knowing he wasn't going to receive an answer, Marcus looked deep into the eyes of the man he was about to execute and asked him, "What have you done to deserve this fate?" He was beginning to sense that this may be an innocent man. Unable to help him, Marcus winced in pain as this man's cross slid ever so slightly, pressing the crown of thorns further into His scalp. The prisoner struggled with His balance, trying hard to keep His cross from falling to the ground while still resting on one knee.

As the moments passed in silence, another soldier riding a horse yelled, "MARCUS! KEEP HIM MOVING!" Marcus dug deep into his soul, gaining the

necessary strength to carry on. Soon, Marcus found someone to carry the cross for Him. This man also struggled while the two men stood and lifted the cross, resting it on their shoulders. It was heavy and awkward to move, dragging behind them, digging into the sand and gravel. While they pressed on, a cloud of dust trailed behind them. Some ridiculed the prisoner, and others struck Him. Some offered Him wine, which He refused. Yet, even others worshiped Him in a mockery; all the while, He pressed on. Then the prisoner spoke to the women who were mourning and lamenting Him, saying, "Daughters do not weep for Me" (Luke 23:28).

The two men collapsed in exhaustion when they finally reached their destination. As they lay on the ground, the cross rested on them. The other soldiers pulled the two men from underneath it, helping them to their feet. Then standing on His own, the prisoner willingly laid Himself on the cross.

Marcus once again found himself looking into the eyes of this Man. However, this time, he had a nail and a mallet in his hands. Then pressing the nail firmly against the condemned Man's flesh, Marcus raised the mallet and with a series of swift blows... BANG—BANG—BANG! "Andrea! Andrea, are you in there?" yelled Janet MacArthur, Andrea's mother, while she pounded on her daughter's bedroom door. Then Janet shouted, "The service should have already started!" Andrea was confident that she had set her alarm clock the night before. Janet banged on her daughter's bedroom door once again. BANG—BANG—BANG! "Andrea! Andrea, do you hear me! Wake up! Wake up, girl! We need to get to the church. Everyone is there waiting for you." As Andrea woke from her dream, she looked at her clock, realizing that she should be standing at the altar looking into the eyes of her groom. Panic set in as she again heard her mother yelling from outside her door, "Andrea, where's your dress? We need your dress! Do you hear me? We need to leave now!"

Wearing only one flip-flop and carrying her wedding dress on one arm with her high heel shoes and make-up bag on the other. Andrea ran to the car where her mother was waiting with her foot on the break. Janet sped off before Andrea could even shut the car door. Andrea said, "Mom, you need to—Ugh—oh, Mom, that was a big pothole—slow down!" "Slow down! You are late for your own wedding and you want me to slow down!" Janet said. "Mom... "Don't mom me! There are over a hundred people at the church waiting for us!" Then Janet looked at her daughter, while taking her eyes off the road, and said, "You have less than five minutes to get your wedding dress on." Then as she turned onto the main highway, she hit a curb, losing a hub cap while blowing through a four-way stop sign.

After Andrea put her wedding dress on, Janet turned the car sharply into the church parking lot. Andrea held on for dear life as she put on her high-heeled shoes. At the same time, the tires slid across the pavement, sending out a screech, announcing to the guests in the sanctuary that the two women had just arrived. Janet put the car in park, and Andrea grabbed the rearview mirror to check her make-up one last time. Holding her wedding dress off the pavement, the two women ran to the church. Racing through the covered walkway, Andrea said, "Mom, I need to talk to you about a dream I had this morning." Almost sprinting, they approached the foyer door, where a man held it open for them. Inside, Andrea saw her father, Kenny Michaels; just then, the pipe organ began to play. Andrea's father asked, "Are you ready, Dear?" Extending his arm and locking arms with her, he escorted her to the altar. Then partway down the aisle, while looking back at her mother, Andrea said with her eyes, "I need to talk to you."

A few minutes later, Andrea said, "I do." "Well, son, you may finally kiss your bride," the minister said. Andrea's husband leaned in and kissed his beautiful wife.

Later the two women finally got a quiet moment to talk at the reception. Janet said, "Andrea, we may have gotten off to a late start, but that sure was a beautiful wedding." Then she asked her daughter, "So, Mrs. Peterson, what is it that you so desperately wanted to talk to me about?" Once again, the two women were interrupted, but this time by the tapping of the crystal glassware, so the bride and groom kissed one more time.

The Cabin in the Deep Dark Woods 2 ~ the first four chapters only

Chapter 2 ~ Sunday
Mr. and Mrs. Peterson

Mr. Peterson asked, "Mrs. Peterson, are you about ready?" "Almost Mr. Peterson," replied Andrea. The newlyweds were both giggling at calling themselves Mr. and Mrs. Peterson that morning following their wedding. They were getting ready to head out to the Cabin in the Deep Dark Woods for their honeymoon.

The company that Mr. Peterson worked for, Wesley Brothers Construction, had a contract with the state parks department to work on the abandoned mine and the surrounding area. They had been working on this project for the last several months and were almost finished. With the deadline fast approaching and Mr. Peterson being the superintendent, the President of the company, Jack Bradford, had decided to put the couple up in the Cabin for two weeks. It's known as the Cabin in the Deep Dark Woods. That's what they call it at the construction company. It's actually called the Cabin in the Way, part of a larger piece of property that belongs to the state parks department. Mr. Peterson would lead the construction crew during the first week, and the second was reserved for the newlyweds' honeymoon. Andrea was not okay with this arrangement until Mr. Bradford decided to pay for their stay at the Cabin. When she didn't smile right away at the meeting, he quickly added, "And I'll provide all the food as well."

Mr. Bradford knew how valuable Mr. Peterson was to that project, so he was determined to keep Andrea happy. Andrea was looking forward to doing some reading and hiking in the woods, a week by herself, some alone time, as she called it. Knowing after almost a year of wedding planning, she could use it.

"The truck is packed. Are you ready, Honey?" Andrea heard the question, but her mind was drifting back to her dream of the man who nailed the hands of Jesus to the cross. "Where would this dream have gone if Mom wouldn't have interrupted?" Then she thought of the mallet hitting the head of the nail and whispered, "His eyes, it wasn't only Marcus' eyes that Jesus pierced; it was mine as well." Thinking more about the dream, she realized when Marcus looked into the eyes of Jesus, he saw the essence of holiness and the purity in His Spirit. "What I saw was hope, faith, and love," she thought.

BANG-BANG-BANG sounded a knock on her door. "Andrea, can you hear me? We need to go," Mr. Peterson said. Realizing she was once again back in that dream, she said, "I'll be ready in just a minute." Rushing over to the mirror, she put a beautiful white bow in her hair. Coming out of the bedroom, her husband looked at her and said, "You look lovely; now we need to go." He picked her up, putting her over his shoulder, and carried her to the truck. She giggled all the way, kicking her feet like she was really trying to escape.

As they pulled out of the driveway with a trailer in tow, Andrea took a good look at her beautiful new home with the white picket fence outlining the front yard. She began to daydream about the children they would one day have and maybe a dog and a cat too. She was confident that a great life lay ahead for them, but another thought raced through her mind. Looking back at a time in her life when she was devastated by her parents' divorce, she thought, "How will I ever break that chain?" Then, returning to reality, she pressed the thought of her parents' divorce out of her head. Looking over at her husband, she said, "There's nothing a girl likes better than taking the company pick-up truck on her honeymoon." "Your right," he said, adding, "but you have to admit, not every girl gets to use the company credit card to buy all the gas." Andrea smiled, thinking how lucky she was to have married such a good man.

Several hours later, the Petersons arrived at the Edwardsville Ranger Station. Mr. Peterson had to check in with the staff to complete the reservation paperwork. "Honey, isn't it beautiful out here?" Mr. Peterson asked. Andrea began to take in the beauty of her surroundings, seeing the mountain tops that seemed to go on forever. "Andrea, I'll be a little while checking in if you want to go for a walk," he said. Just then, her phone rang. "Not much chance of cell service up hear Ma'am," one of the park rangers said, adding, "you might want to take that call."

Saying, "Hello," as she answered her phone, noticing it was her mother who was calling. After a few moments of small talk, Janet asked, "What was it you so desperately wanted to talk to me about at your wedding?" Andrea went into detail, telling her mother everything that happened in her dream. Then she said, "Mom, the man who nailed Jesus to the cross in my dream was Marcus." Janet interrupted her daughter sharply, saying, "Let me be clear with you, young lady, I know a good man when I see one, and Marcus is a good man. Don't begin to doubt your husband, especially on your honeymoon." Then Janet began to describe her first meeting with Marcus at the restaurant that day by saying: "Remember he was the last one to the table because he helped that elderly woman up after she fell in the parking lot, tripping over a parking curb. Her family had to cancel their dinner reservation with her because of a family emergency. It was Marcus who brought her to our table to have dinner with us. Andrea, do you remember what day that was?" "Yes, Mother, I remember; it was Mother's Day." "That's right, Dear, it was. I remember crying on my menu and thinking that Marcus is a very good man. And don't you forget that this week!" There was a long pause, and Andrea said, "Hello—hello—Mom, are you there?" The same park ranger walked by and said, "I've never seen anyone get cell service up here before."

Just then, Marcus Peterson walked out of the ranger station. Looking at his wife, he said, "Andrea, are you ready to head to the cabin now?" Looking up from her cell phone, she noticed that the ranger had loaded all the luggage and equipment onto the John Deere and hooked the trailer up to it while she was talking on the phone.

The Cabin in the Deep Dark Woods 2 ~ the first four chapters only

Chapter 3 ~ Sunday
The John Deere

Wearing his sunglasses, Marcus was standing in front of an old hardwood bench on the ranger station's wrap-around front porch. Andrea took one look at her new husband and thought, "Wow, Mom's right as rain; that sure is a good man." "Honey," Marcus said, as he walked her way, "are you ready? Our ride is about to leave." "Hop on up here, Ma'am, Ranger Lucas Ward at your service. Welcome to Edwardsville. I'll have you two love birds to the cabin in less than five minutes; it's about a twenty-minute hike if you choose to walk." Marcus helped Andrea into the back seat.

"HOLD ON TIGHT," Lucas said. He pushed the gas pedal all the way to the floor, saying, "I hope you don't mind going fast!" Then he hit a pothole while leaving the ranger station parking area. Andrea had a flashback of her mom driving her to the wedding yesterday morning. Holding on for dear life, she remembered her mom hitting that pothole. Andrea thought, "My mother must have taught this man how to drive!" Over the noise of the motor, Lucas yelled, "I know this place like the back of my hand." Referring to the fact that he had been a ranger for the state parks department for many years and knew every trail backward and forward. Then he said, "You can always count on me." And turning around while driving, he began talking to Andrea, saying, "Ma'am, we're taking the second marked trail to the cabin. If you look over there, you can see one of the adits." Then he negotiated a sharp curve, hardly slowing down. Then he explained, "An adit is an entrance to the mine. Over there is one of the discarded rock piles from years gone by."

Continuing with his tour, Lucas said, "Up ahead is the red covered bridge. The creek sure is getting high this spring; it should crest sometime tomorrow. We gotta be careful around the creek," Lucas warned. Continuing his speech all the way to the cabin, explaining in detail the third marked trail that led to the abandoned miners' village. It ran along the creek bank, where some people had found ancient Indian relics, where the rocks were, while on their way to the miners' village. "We are on the straightaway now and will be at the cabin soon," Lucas yelled as he was driving through an open field at top speed. Lucas said, "Yes sir, I'm a praying man; I gotta be the way I drive around these trails. The Lord has kept His hand on me over the years." A few minutes later, Lucas said, "Well, it looks like we are here." He parked the John Deere by the stone wall attached to the front of the Cabin. "Over there is the first marked trail. It leads to the cabin parking area on Sandrock Creek Boulevard," At that, Lucas completed his self-imposed tour guide session of Edwardsville.

Andrea walked into the cabin and noticed how plain it was, all open except the bathroom. Lucas entered the

The Cabin in the Deep Dark Woods 2

cabin with her luggage and noticed how disappointed she looked. He told her that the cabin had been built as a church many years ago. He said, "It was not finished until the town of Edwardsville decided to make it into a one-room schoolhouse years later. Now it's this quaint little cabin out here in the middle of nowhere." Lucas realized that he hadn't made the idea of staying there any better for her, so he headed back outside to help Marcus.

"Let me help you," Lucas said while Marcus unhooked the trailer from the John Deere. "Boss, I'll be back here bright and early tomorrow morning to pick you up," The two men said goodbye and shook hands. Then he got back in the "Deere," at least that's what Lucas called it, and sped off.

Andrea walked out of the cabin to where Marcus was securing the trailer and said, "Honey, does anyone else know that man drives like a maniac. It's a wonder he didn't kill us." Looking at her watch, she said, "And we've only been married for twenty-one hours." Marcus responded, "I know, but he's my right-hand man on this project. If it wasn't for his knowledge of the property, we would have had to postpone the wedding. He is worth his weight in gold to me." "Well, then it's a good thing he's a little man because we couldn't afford him if he were any bigger," Andrea said while turning around to go back into the Cabin. Marcus asked, "What are your plans for tomorrow while I'm working with the crew?" "I think I'll go for a walk and see what kind of trouble I can get myself into." Then she asked, "Why don't you spend the day with me?"

tempting her new husband to call in sick. Marcus said, "You know I can't do that, but it's really tempting as he chased her to the front door of the cabin, where she stopped. Marcus instinctively picked up his beautiful new wife and carried her across the threshold. Placing her back on her feet, he kissed her and confessed his love to her.

Later that evening, Andrea was unpacking her bags, and she took out her yellow hiking hat and hung it on a hook. Marcus said, "Honey, are you really going to wear that silly yellow hat around here? "Why yes I am; this is my favorite hiking hat. I'm sure you will come to love it just as I do," Andrea said. Then she thought, "Marcus, do you believe in God?"

All was quiet at the Cabin in the Deep Dark Woods. However, a couple of men wearing hooded cloaks with their faces concealed, having glowing eyes, kept a watch over things outside.

The Cabin in the Deep Dark Woods 2 ~ the first four chapters only

Chapter 4 ~ Monday
The Rocks Cry Out

While Andrea slept, she was awakened by the sound of the speeding John Deere zooming by the front of the cabin. Andrea said, "Marcus, you need to do something about that man and his driving; it's not even 6:30 yet!" "Honey, I gotta go. I'll see you tonight," Marcus said as he kissed her goodbye. "Hey! You didn't tell me where you're working today," Andrea said. She sat up in bed, anticipating an answer. "We are going to be working on one of the rock piles on the other side of the ranger station," Marcus said as he gave her another kiss before he walked out the door.

"Good morning, Boss. Is that little lady still sleeping?" Lucas asked. From inside the cabin, Andrea yelled, "Not anymore, thank you very much!" However, neither of the two men heard her. Marcus and Lucas walked to the John Deere, and Andrea overheard Lucas ask, "Boss, where do you want to go first?" After the two men drove off, Andrea could not get back to sleep. She rose to the aroma of freshly made coffee that blended perfectly with the fresh mountain air. Andrea thought, "How nice of Marcus to make me coffee this morning."

After two cups of coffee and a filling breakfast, Andrea laced up her hiking boots. She had decided that it was the perfect day to hike down to the abandoned miners' village. "I sure hope I can find some kind of ancient artifact to remember this trip by," she thought. Before long, she had crossed the red covered bridge making her way down the third marked trail. Soon, she saw what she thought was an ancient Indian arrowhead close to the creek bank between some rocks. Then carefully making her way to the water's edge walking on the rocks, she reached down to pick it up. Disregarding Lucas's warning the day before about the dangers of the rising creek with its fast-moving water, she slipped on a wet rock falling into the creek.

Over at the construction site, Marcus oversaw his crew of seven personnel while clearing out an abandoned rock pile. Suddenly, a man wearing a hooded cloak walked up behind him and said with the voice of holiness, "Behold, the rocks cry out." Looking behind himself and seeing no one, Marcus yelled, "ANDREA!" Hearing the desperation in his voice, Lucas ran over to the John Deere. Looking at Marcus, he exclaimed, "THE CREEK! WE NEED TO GET DOWN TO THE CREEK!"

"HOLD ON TIGHT," Lucas yelled as he raced the John Deere past the ranger station toward the red covered bridge. Then he turned onto the third marked trail toward the abandoned miners' village. Parking the John Deer, the two men dismounted and ran down to the creek where the water was raging. Marcus yelled, "That's Andrea's yellow hat, oh my God, she's in the water!" Lucas shouted, "Get back in the Deere; I know where she's going to land!" The two men sped off in the direction of the main highway. Lucas grabbed his radio and said, "Ranger Lucas Ward to base." Base replied, "Base here, Ranger Ward proceed with your message." Lucas said, "Base, we have a possible Signal 7 in the creek. Send all available personnel to intercept at the Sandrock Creek Boulevard Bridge." Base replied, "Base to all personnel, proceed to assist Ranger Ward at the Sandrock Creek Boulevard Bridge. This is an all-hands incident!" As Lucas hurried to the intercept point, Marcus asked him, "Lucas, what's a signal 7?" Lucas responded to his question by saying, "I know a shortcut down an unmarked trail. Hold on tight; it's going to get really bumpy!" The two men raced down a steep rocky embankment. Afterward, Lucas turned the John Deere onto the main highway and said, "Up ahead is the bridge; that's where we're headed."

While she floated down the creek, Andrea suddenly realized her feet were firmly planted on the ground. She was wearing a shiny white gown and was completely dry. She found herself standing in a beautiful warm garden and began to walk. She noticed various types of trees that she had never seen before. Soon, she heard a voice from behind her, saying, "Andrea, I am always with you and your children." Andrea turned around and saw a man walking toward her having a light emanating from his center like the glory of God. The man extended his hand toward her and said, "Andrea, come, take my hand and walk with me."

The man and Andrea walked through the garden for some time. Then He began to speak to her again, saying, "There are many trees in my garden that are pleasant to the sight and good for food. I want to inform you about those two trees that you see in the center" (Genesis 2:9). The man showed Andrea two trees that were straight ahead. Then he pointed to the beautiful one and said, "That tree is the tree of life, and all who eat of it will live forever" (Genesis 3:22). "I will be giving you instruction on the tree of life soon," the man said. "I have brought you here to talk to you about the tree that is next to it. It's called the tree of the knowledge of good and evil." While he was talking to Andrea, she was looking at the tree next to the beautiful one. She was puzzled and asked the man, "Why would anyone eat the fruit of that tree?" The man began to explain to her why she had been brought there, saying, "You see Andrea, your husband is eating daily from that tree. As the name implies, it is the tree of the knowledge of good and evil. Your husband is feeding on the good side of that tree. I will shortly give you insight about your children and how their lives will turn out while your husband, Marcus, continues to eat from the good side of that tree." Andrea asked, "But when will I receive this insight? The man said, "It will begin tomorrow morning, very early."

After they had walked in the garden for a fair amount of time, the man said, "Andrea, it is time for you to go back now." As Andrea looked down, she noticed that she was again wearing her hiking outfit and soaking wet. When the man let go of her hand, she saw the nail print in His hand. Looking directly into His eyes, Andrea said, to Him, "You're the One that Marcus nailed to the cross in my dream, aren't you?" "No, Andrea, it was you. You were the one who nailed Me to the cross," the Man said while looking deep into her eyes. She felt more love emanating from this Man than she had ever felt before.

Suddenly, Andrea had this deep awareness that she could no longer breathe. Then the Man said, "Andrea, I have one more word for you regarding the tree of the knowledge of good and evil..." Andrea thought, "I really hope You hurry up because I am soaking wet, I am chilled to the bone, I can no longer breathe, and I feel as if I'm fading fast." Then the Man continued, "Don't look at the fruit of that tree, don't touch it, and don't eat it (Genesis 3:2-6). Andrea, do you understand what I have told you?" As He finished asking her that question, He moved ever closer to her until He finally placed His mouth on hers. Now holding her up with His arms because she had become entirely limp, the Man breathed the breath of life back into her lungs.

Less than a minute after turning onto Sandrock Creek Boulevard, Lucas and Marcus arrived at the intercept point. Making their way down the embankment, they were the first ones to reach Andrea. She was lying face down on the sandy beach exactly where Lucas had predicted she would land. Marcus knelt down and embraced his wife, and then she opened her eyes and began to breathe again. Lucas caught a glimpse of the Man with the hooded cloak as He made his way back into the deep dark woods. Then, the

Edwardsville Volunteer Fire Company number One arrived on the scene with the rangers and the construction workers.

The End ~ The Cabin in the Deep Dark Woods 2 ~ The Spirit and the Bride—the first four chapters only.

The full 26 chapter novel, *The Cabin in the Deep Dark Woods 2 ~ The Spirit and the Bride*—is available on <u>Amazon.com</u>

Book Overview:

With the wedding fast approaching and the latest construction project facing an imminent deadline, Marcus is faced with a decision to postpone the wedding or incorporate his work into his honeymoon. Marcus and his crew must remove a time capsule buried during a cave-in at the Edwardsville mine many years ago. However, there is a more pressing issue on Marcus's mind. What effect will a secret from his past have on Andrea, his beautiful new bride? Her faith will be tested and challenged as his sin from the past is uncovered. Will his construction crew be a help or a hindrance in this endeavor? Join these two honeymooners as they dig into their past, their future, and the mine at the Cabin in the Deep Dark Woods. There are discussion questions and devotionals at the end of each chapter.

Appendix A

The Minister of the Holy Spirit
The Holy Spirit on Training Wheels

The Fear of the Lord is the beginning of Knowledge and Wisdom—Proverbs 1:7 & 9:10.

This study is intended to introduce you to a lifelong commitment to Jesus Christ. It should be started on day one and continue through day ninety in order. It is intended to allow the Holy Spirit to come alive and speak to you, acting like the Holy Spirit on training wheels. There will be individuals who discover while reading their Bibles that they were never born again. The Holy Spirit will begin to work on you, bringing you to the place where you can receive that inner peace that surpasses all understanding. The Holy Spirit is the life force behind this study.

After completion, each participant should read the entire Bible by following a one-year reading plan or utilize a one-year Bible (recommended). Before you get started, there is one more instruction to undertake. You will need to get a separate notepad and journal your thoughts from the book of Proverbs. For example, you will be instructed to read a passage from Proverbs that correlates to the calendar date. (e.g., it is September 28: therefore, you would read Proverbs chapter 28 that day). You may read the same chapter in Proverbs multiple times throughout your reading. When the ninety days are completed, question God about all the chapters in Proverbs you did not read. This strange way of reading Proverbs is an intended design of this study.

After completion, and while reading through your Bible, pay particular attention to Job, Psalms, Proverbs, Ecclesiastes, and the Song of Solomon for the promises of God. Begin by opening in prayer, and then read Acts 12:5, Romans 1:9, I Thessalonians 5:16-22, and II Timothy 1:3-4.

Psalms 90:12 Teach us to number our days and recognize how few they are; help us to spend them as we should [TLB].

Day zero is your foundational day.

Day 0 Isaiah 52:13-15 and Isaiah 53:1-12. His visage was so marred more than any man.

Day 1 Acts 17: they searched the Scriptures daily to find out whether these things were so.

Day 2 The Proverbs chapter that correlates to today's date.

Day 3 Joshua 4 & Matthew 3: the stones from the Jordon River.

Day 4 Matthew 5: the Beatitudes and Jesus came to fulfill the law.

Day 5 The Proverbs chapter that correlates to today's date.

Appendix

Day 6 Acts 1 & 2: the Holy Spirit is the Promise of the Father.

Day 7 Acts 3 & 4: Peter heals a man and then delivers a sermon.

Day 8 Acts 5 & 6: Gamaliel & the apostles, Steven full of faith and the Holy Spirit.

Day 9 Acts 7 & 8: Stevens's sermon, Samaria receives the Holy Spirit.

Day 10 Acts 9 & 10: Saul's conversion and Cornelius filled with the Holy Spirit.

Day 11 Acts 11 & 12: Peter defends going to the Gentiles. Peter escapes from prison.

Day 12 The Proverbs chapter that correlates to today's date.

Day 13 Revelation 1, 2, and 3: John's vision and the seven letters to the seven churches.

Day 14 Exodus 14 & I Corinthians 10: the children of Israel coming out of Egypt.

Day 15 The Proverbs chapter that correlates to today's date.

Day 16 Luke 1: John the Baptist was filled with the Holy Spirit in the womb.

Day 17 Matthew 14: Jesus walks on the sea.

Day 18 The Proverbs chapter that correlates to today's date.

Day 19 Mark 4: the parable of the sower/four soils.

Day 20 I Peter 1: the angels desire to understand the gospel message of salvation.

Day 21 The Proverbs chapter that correlates to today's date.

Day 22 II Kings 4: the widow's jar of oil overflows, and a son is born to a barren woman.

Day 23 II Corinthians 12: I shall mourn for those who have not repented of their sin.

Day 24 The Proverbs chapter that correlates to today's date.

Day 25 Psalms 119:1-56: blessed are those who walk in the law of the Lord.

Day 26 Psalms 119:57-112: You are my portion, O Lord.

Day 27 Psalms 119:113-176: I long for Your salvation, O Lord.

Day 28 The Proverbs chapter that correlates to today's date.

Day 29 Zachariah 3: the vision of the high priest standing before the Lord.

Day 30 Luke 2: the Child, His name was called Jesus.

Day 31 The Proverbs chapter that correlates to today's date.

Day 32 I Corinthians 12: For by one Spirit, we were all baptized into one body.

Day 33 Jeremiah 33: David & the Levites shall never lack a man to stand before God.

Day 34 The Proverbs chapter that correlates to today's date.

Day 35 Galatians 5: But the fruit of the Spirit is love, joy, peace…

Day 36 Jeremiah 35: Jonadab shall not want a man to stand before Me forever.

Day 37 The Proverbs chapter that correlates to today's date.

Day 38 I Corinthians 13: but the greatest of these is love.

Day 39 Psalms 51: Create in me a clean heart, O God.

Day 40 Matthew 13: the parable of the sower/four soils.

Day 41 Luke 3: the Holy Spirit descended upon Jesus.

Day 42 The Proverbs chapter that correlates to today's date.

Day 43 Genesis 14 & Psalms 110: order of Melchizedek king of Salem priest of God Most High.

Appendix

Day 44 Hebrews 5, 6, and 7: the order of Melchizedek king of Salem priest of God Most High.

Day 45 II Corinthians 3: you are an epistle of Christ, written by the Spirit of the living God.

Day 46 Luke 4: The Spirit of the LORD is upon Me to preach the gospel to the poor.

Day 47 Matthew 7: I never knew you; depart from Me, you who practice lawlessness!

Day 48 The Proverbs chapter that correlates to today's date.

Day 49 II Timothy 2 & Hebrews 11: study the word of God and believe in faith that God exists.

Day 50 The Proverbs chapter that correlates to today's date.

Day 51 Exodus 3: Moses and the burning bush—Holy ground.

Day 52 The Proverbs chapter that correlates to today's date.

Day 53 Joshua 5: Commander of the army of the LORD—Holy ground.

Day 54 The Proverbs chapter that correlates to today's date.

Day 55 Luke 5: "Depart from me, for I am a sinful man, O Lord!"

Day 56 The Proverbs chapter that correlates to today's date.

Day 57 Matthew 26: Peter denies Jesus three times and then weeps bitterly.

Day 58 The Proverbs chapter that correlates to today's date.

Day 59 Mark 16: but go, tell His disciples—and Peter.

Day 60 The Proverbs chapter that correlates to today's date.

Day 61 John 21: feed My lambs, tend My sheep, and feed My sheep—Peter restored.

Day 62 The Proverbs chapter that correlates to today's date.

Day 63 Matthew 20: can you be baptized with the baptism that I am baptized with?

Day 64 The Proverbs chapter that correlates to today's date.

Day 65 Zephaniah 3: I will restore to the people a pure language.

Day 66 The Proverbs chapter that correlates to today's date.

Day 67 Joel 2: your sons & daughters shall prophesy, and your old men shall dream dreams.

Day 68 Matthew 28: Go therefore and make disciples of all the nations baptizing them...

Day 69 The Proverbs chapter that correlates to today's date.

Day 70 Luke 8: the parable of the sower/four soils.

Day 71 Acts 19: baptized in the name of the Lord Jesus, the Holy Spirit came upon them.

Day 72 The Proverbs chapter that correlates to today's date.

Day 73 Romans 6: Christ was raised from the dead by the glory of the Father.

Day 74 The Proverbs chapter that correlates to today's date.

Day 75 Luke 23: "Father, forgive them, for they do not know what they do."

Day 76 I Corinthians 1: He who glories, let him glory in the Lord.

Day 77 The Proverbs chapter that correlates to today's date.

Appendix

Day 78 Ephesians 6: put on the whole armor of God, and praying always in the Spirit.

Day 79 The Proverbs chapter that correlates to today's date.

Day 80 Ezekiel 36: I will give you a new heart and put a new spirit within you.

Day 81 Matthew 17: Jesus was transfigured before them.

Day 82 The Proverbs chapter that correlates to today's date.

Day 83 John 3: unless one is born of water and the Spirit, he cannot enter the kingdom of God.

Day 84 I Peter 4: If the righteous are scarcely saved, what about the ungodly and the sinner?

Day 85 The Proverbs chapter that correlates to today's date.

Day 86 Luke 24: the law of Moses, the prophets, and the Psalms must be fulfilled.

Day 87 Psalms 139: I was made in secret, and skillfully wrought in the lowest parts of the earth.

Day 88 II Peter 1: holy men of God spoke as they were moved by the Holy Spirit.

Day 89 The Proverbs chapter that correlates to today's date.

Day 90 Revelation 22: and the Spirit and the bride say, "Come!"

When finished, read Psalms 22: Jesus on the cross.

Appendix B
Non-Believer's Challenge
A Sixty-Day Study

Introduction: Have you ever wondered why so many people believe in God? Why not spend every other day reading the Bible? For this study, you will read various passages from the Bible for 15 to 20 minutes on even days of the month. On odd days, you will journal for 15 to 20 minutes about YOUR belief that God is NOT real. This 60-day study aims to spend your even days reading the Bible and your odd days journaling your thoughts. Particularly your thoughts about NOT believing in God.

If you DON'T believe in God, this study is for you. If you believe God to be a myth, it should be worth your time to prove it. Another aspect of this study is being true to yourself, specifically your journaling on the odd days. If someone cannot be true to themselves, who can they be true to? If you have two odd days in a row, simply journal for both of those days.

At the end of the 60 days comes a unique feature of this study. You will read your journal, then answer the question: Do I believe in God? If you answer YES, you may choose to attend a local church, seek out a friend who is a believer, or just continue reading your Bible. If you answer NO, I encourage you to seek out believers and question them about their faith.

Non-Believer's Challenge Passage List.
1. Psalms 19, I Kings 18, Psalms 64, Acts 17:11.
2. Psalms 51, Zechariah 3, Psalms 35, Zechariah 12:10.
3. Psalms 72, John 3, Psalms 8, Matthew 3:11.

Appendix

4. Psalms 23, I Peter 3, Psalms 59, Matthew 9:13.
5. Psalms 1, I John 1, Psalms 55, Mark 1:4.
6. Psalms 123, Luke 1, Psalms 70, I Timothy 4:1-3.
7. Psalms 91, Proverbs 3, Psalms 68, Mark 2:17.
8. Psalms 73, Job 1, Psalms 84, II Timothy 3:5.
9. Psalms 90, Matthew 16, Psalms 112, Luke 3:8.
10. Psalms 107, Job 32, Psalms 34, Luke 5:32.
11. Psalms 69, Luke 23, Psalms 100, Luke 15:7.
12. Psalms 2, Judges 13, Psalms 13, John 1:12.
13. Psalms 110, Exodus 3, Psalms 85, Luke 24:7.
14. Psalms 20, Joshua 5, Psalms 95, Acts 5:31.
15. Psalms 9, Genesis 3, Psalms 97, Acts 11:18.
16. Psalms 135, I Timothy 2, Psalms 48, Acts 13:22-24.
17. Psalms 22, Hebrews 11, Psalms 103, Acts 19:4.
18. Psalms 26, Habakkuk 2, Psalms 144, Rev. 2:7.
19. Psalms 41, Romans 1, Psalms 86, Acts 20:21.
20. Psalms 79, Galatians 3, Psalms 139, Acts 26:19-20.
21. Psalms 92, Hebrews 10, Psalms 128, Romans 2.1-4.
22. Psalms 80, Hosea 14, Psalms 37, Romans 11:29.
23. Psalms 50, Isaiah 52.13-15, Isaiah 53, Psalms 98.
24. Psalms 32, Joel 2, Psalms 150, II Timothy 3:7.
25. Psalms 66, Deuteronomy 7, Psalms 13, II Corinthians 7:9-10.
26. Psalms 82, Ecclesiastes 2, Psalms 121, II Timothy 2:24-26.
27. Psalms 14, Lamentations 3, Psalms 54, Hebrews 6:1.
28. Psalms 104, James 5, Psalms 74, Malachi 3:10.
29. Psalms 126, Matthew 3, Psalms 5, Hosea 13:14.
30. Psalms 42, I Corinthians 15, II Peter 3.9. Psalms 19.

Appendix C
Suicide Journal

Instruction to the Way of Life
Note: Italics are utilized to indicate scripture.

The goal of the Suicide Journal Instruction to the Way of Life, is to extend the life of a desperate person by five days, by journaling their feelings and reading their responses on subsequent days of the journal process.

This Journal Is A Three-Step Process

Step one: admit to yourself that you have suicidal thoughts.

Step two: get a pen and paper. Write on anything that you can, even the wall or the mirror.

Step three: write down your thoughts on paper and answer question 1, question 2, and question 3.

Question 1. To be asked on journal day one. Can I wait until tomorrow to take my life?

Question 2. To be asked on journal day two through four. Upon reading my journal notes from yesterday, is my situation any less desperate?

Question 3. To be asked on journal day five. Upon review of my journal notes: is there an improvement in my will to live? And is there a glimmer of hope that my life has value?

Further instruction of the process: Your life has value. Life is what you make of it. What you put into it is the very thing that you get out of it. *John 15:22 [KJV] If I had not come and spoken unto them, they had not had sin: but now they have no cloak for their sin.* In this verse, Jesus speaks of a cloak or a hiding place. A cloak is something that conceals or hides. The fact that you have gotten this far in the Suicide Journal shows you have become honest with yourself. You have removed the cloak, your hiding place, that the only answer to your problem is suicide. There must be another answer to the question: "Should I take my own life today?"

The first question that needs to be asked: "Is there any value to my life?" **The second question is:** "Can I add value to my life?" **The answer to question one must be YES.** All life comes from God, and that alone **QUALIFIES YOU AS VALUABLE. The answer to question two must also be YES.** Adding value to your life is a daily process. You are the only one who can do this. You must understand that your thoughts are trying to kill you, and this is not of God. Mankind was created in God's Own image, and any opinion contrary to that is not of God. If while asking yourself, is there a glimmer of hope that my life has value and you said no, then you must understand that Jesus loves you anyway. Jesus also went to the cross and died for you. Cry out to God in your darkest hour, and He will hear your cry.

Understandably, you may not be able to see tomorrow as a new day, but the love of God is everlasting. I hope this helps as no one but Jesus can fully understand your situation and have an answer to help you overcome your darkest hour. Seek Jesus, and you will find Him. Ask Jesus, and He will comfort you. Pray to Jesus, and He will hear you. When you are talking to Jesus, don't be afraid to pour your heart out and let your tears flow like a river. Jesus loves you.

John 1:1 In the beginning was the Word, and the Word was with God, and the Word was God.

John 6:57 "As the living Father sent Me, and I live because of the Father, so he who feeds on Me will live because of Me.

Suicide Journal Instructions
DAY ONE

Question 1. Can I wait until tomorrow to take my life? This answer will have to come from the heart, and a NO answer must be dismissed. You must be strong and say, "YES, I CAN LIVE ANOTHER DAY."

DAY TWO

Question 2. Upon reading my journal notes from yesterday, is my situation any less desperate? Your life must not be as hopeless on day two as it was on day one because you made it through the night. What did you write in your journal yesterday? Please read it and re-read it; you are the author. Rebuild your life based on the value that you have found between day one and day two.

Appendix

DAY THREE

Continue to expand your thoughts and be honest with yourself. A big part of getting rid of suicidal thoughts is to be honest with yourself. If you tell yourself that you have no value long enough, eventually you will start to believe it. Truth begins within and expands to the outside in the form of value. Self-value and God are the cure to suicidal thoughts.

DAY FOUR

This is a reinforcement of day three. If you are on day four, then you have added four days of value to your life.

DAY FIVE

Question 3. To be asked on journal day five. Upon review of my journal notes, is there an improvement in my will to live? And is there a glimmer of hope that my life has value.

At this point in the journal process, you should have five days of journal notes to review. That is five days of value that you have added to your life. If you have become honest with yourself, you now have your honest opinion to draw from. This journal is the person you have become over the last five days. You have become honest with yourself and have put aside your suicidal thoughts for the previous five days. Take council in your journal by using your own words to find value in your life. If you take your life, you will no longer have it, and you can never get it back. Be warned that you are weak and in need of help. At the very least, you will need to continue to journal, reading, and re-

reading your thoughts. Just because you made it to day five or day six doesn't mean that you can't go back to your darkest hour. Press on and add value to your life every day through honesty and truth.

John 15:26 But when the Helper comes, whom I shall send to you from the Father, the Spirit of truth who proceeds from the Father, He will testify of Me.

Remember, suicide is an act of a person intentionally taking their own life. If the act of suicide is never started, then the act of suicide can never be finished. Life moves on, move along with it, and begin to direct your path in honesty and truth. The new beginning starts here and now.

The next step is to seek professional help.

National Suicide Prevention lifeline: 1-800-273-TALK (8255)

Thank You from the Author

Thank you for purchasing *Ye Three Men ~ Bonus Edition*. If you would like to be included in the newsletter, please send an email to:

TheCabin@turnifyouwill.org
TheCabinInTheDeepDarkWoods.com

I hope you enjoyed reading the bonus edition of ***The Cabin in the Deep Dark Woods ~ A Discerner of the Heart*** (&) ***The Cabin in the Deep Dark Woods 2 ~ The Spirit and the Bride.*** If you enjoyed these samples of the first four chapters of each book, they are available on Amazon in paperback and eBook. There are twenty-six chapters in each book with discussion questions and a devotional at the end of each chapter.

So, Please be sure to visit The Cabin in the Deep Dark Woods by reading the books in that series:

The Cabin in the Deep Dark Woods—A Discerner of the Heart.
The Cabin in the Deep Dark Woods 2—The Spirit and the Bride.
The Cabin in the Deep Dark Woods 3—Lost in the Way.
Release date late 2021 or early 2022.

I have turned this book into a series; however, they can be read in any order, and each book has new characters. These stories revolve around a place called Edwardsville, where there is a cabin, a mine, and a ranger station.

Other books by the author:
Ye Three Men Devotional Edition: Devotional with Scripture.
In this version, the scriptures are written out in the devotional section. These books are available on Amazon.com

Thank you
Tim Barker

Made in United States
Orlando, FL
06 October 2022